THE END

Thomas F. Smith
and
Shannon Gambino

Grosvenor House
Publishing Limited

This book is published by
Grosvenor House Publishing Ltd
Link House
140 The Broadway, Tolworth, Surrey, KT6 7HT.
www.grosvenorhousepublishing.co.uk

A CIP record for this book
is available from the British Library

ISBN 978-1-78623-565-7

Cover Art: mphillips007, iStock 185115054; D-Keine, iStock 104522789,
94927468; Anagramm, iStock 453241567.
Cover Layout: Shannon Gambino
Co-Author; Editor: Shannon Gambino

For my children:
Ashley, who said she was proud of me for starting this novel.
Caroline, who provided me with her support and assistance.
Brian, who is becoming the man I wish I could have been.

I wanted to make all of you proud of me, and that is the number one reason why I wrote this book. I hope I succeeded.

For my Marine Corps brothers and sisters:
Semper Fi and God bless.

For my friends at the Monmouth County Sheriff's Office:
it was my honor to serve with you for twenty-six years. God bless all of you and keep you safe on the streets.

TABLE OF CONTENTS

AUTHOR'S NOTES

Facts: Yellowstone National Park volcanic eruptions.
Huckleberry Ridge Eruption: 2.1 million years ago
Mesa Falls Eruption: 1.3 million years ago
Lava Creek Eruption: 630,000 years ago

Fact: Bubonic Plague (or Black Death)
Years: 1348 – 1666
Deaths: 75 – 200 million
Believed to have originated in China and Turkistan and then transported to Genoa, Italy, in January 1348, by merchant ships carrying disease-ridden rats.

Fact: Cannibalism
Evidence suggests our ancestors had cannibalistic tendencies dating as far back as 800,000 years ago. Given the right conditions, instincts overcome the aversion to eating human flesh (*long pig* in some regions).
American pioneers in the Donner Party crossing the Sierra Nevada Mountains were said to have resorted to cannibalism to survive when they became snowbound.
The survivors of Uruguayan flight 571 that crashed into the Andes Mountains on October 13, 1972, fed off the flesh of dead passengers until they were rescued seventy-two days later.

– T.S.

Revelation 6:13 – 17, NIV
Then I watched while he broke open the sixth seal, and there was a great earthquake; the sun turned as black as dark sackcloth and the whole moon became like blood. The stars in the sky fell to earth like unripe figs shaken loose from the tree in a strong wind. Then the sky was divided like a torn scroll curling up, and every mountain and island was moved from its place. The Kings of the earth, the nobles, the military officers, the rich, the powerful, and every slave and free person hid themselves in caves and among mountain crags. They cried out to the mountains and the rocks, 'Fall on us and hide us from the face of the one who sits on the throne and from the wrath of the Lamb, because the great day of their wrath has come and who can withstand it?'

PROLOGUE

SOMEWHERE IN AMERICA.

March 28, Easter Sunday, Year of Our Lord, 2032.

The last civilized man left alive in this broken world. He does not know this, of course. How could he? Of the others remaining, their raw survival instincts have relinquished any semblance of humanity. Like a pack of wild dogs, they hunt him until they turn on themselves.

The wind made an eerie, unnatural sound as it moved through the barren branches of the tall, oak trees surrounding his small cabin; another interrupted night of restless sleep. What was it that woke him?

Scratch, scratch.

Softly, he heard it again. Fear can be a funny thing, grabbing you tightly; for some, never letting go ... a lifelong companion.

Outside, the darkness and bitter cold awaited him. The temperature, by his estimate, had been a constant -10 to -20 °F and not likely to get any better. *Hell, it was only the middle of March or early April,* but he did not quite know. Calendars and thermometers were a thing of the past, along with electricity, fuel, and food.

Food.

It had been two days since his last meal. *No, that was a lie.* It was closer to four days. He had to find something to eat today, despite the miserable weather.

As the months passed, the temperatures plummeted. *When was the last time he had seen the sun and moon ... or the sky, for that matter?* More than likely, he wouldn't be alive by August, so why should he worry about it.

Scratch.

Fully awake, his gaze moved to the window of his tiny, temporary hovel. He had stumbled upon the sad shelter, deep in the woods during his endless search for food.

Scratch.

It was nothing more than that damned branch moving against the sole window of the cabin. He had meant to cut it off the old, oak tree but had forgotten. Never-ending frigid temperatures make you forget things and focus solely on the ice, snow, and wind. He hated the idea of getting out of bed. *Bed?* That was a laugh. *More like a pissed-on old mattress with stains from origins he did not even want to imagine*, but he knew he had to stand up and get his blood circulating. The roaring fire he had started before he fell asleep was now only glowing embers and ash, fading into the darkness. He had been a fool to let the fire die out. If he wanted to survive, he had to keep the fire going, but he was too tired. It had been a long journey through the woods and relentless icy wind. It was pure luck that he stumbled upon the abandoned cabin two days prior.

With a great deal of reluctance, he pushed aside his makeshift blankets and swung his legs over the side of the bed. No need to get dressed or put on boots – he always went to bed fully clothed, not only for warmth but for a chance to escape the hunters. There was much more to fear in the woods than cold and starvation.

The day before, he collected as much wood as possible, but water and food were scarce. *Food.* His first priority, though, was getting the fire going again. *God, what he would give for a cup of coffee or even some tea. How long had it been since he had tasted either?*

He had set traps around a small nearby lake, about a quarter of a mile away. The ice on the lake was too thick for fishing, but along the shoreline, he was able to chip through enough to reach the water beneath and fill his canteens. With any luck, he would have meat on his breakfast plate to enjoy with his water.

His to-do list was short for the day: cut down the annoying tree branch and find food. He needed to eat something, anything to quiet the constant grumbling in the pit of his stomach: deer, squirrel, rat, nuts or berries – it made no difference to him. The wind was getting stronger. If he waited any longer, it would be too cold for any wild game to be on the move.

As he added more precious wood to his fire, a movement outside the shack's window caught his eye. He tried to convince himself it was the damned branch, but the prickly hairs on the back of his neck told him otherwise. Reaching under his pillow, he drew out his buck knife. He knew it was hopeless ... the shrouded ones always traveled in packs. The cannibals – the flesh eaters – had found him. The door of the cabin burst open, and he knew no more.

ONE

BROKEN BOW, NEBRASKA.

April 7, 2030.

Raymond B. Smith was a seventy-seven-year-old farmer at the 'ass-end of life,' according to him. As such, few things frightened him, but at the moment, he was damned scared. Rain clouds were forming again. Large, dark clouds – what the weather forecasters liked to call *cumulus clouds*. They claimed to know so much, but he didn't need some fancy man in a three-piece suit to tell him rain was coming. Hell, just looking at the sky, he could figure it out on his own. Most of the time, farmers loved a good cloudburst. It meant much-needed water for crops and livestock. Except his crops were already drowning. Too much damned water was just as bad as too little, perhaps worse.

During dry spells, he pumped the water out to his crops from one of the many wells located around his 200-acre property. He also had Smither's Stream that ran through his acreage as well as the Millers' land. In his lifetime, Smither's Stream had only gone dry once, during the drought of 1969. Those had been tough times, for sure. His father and everyone else in the county had come close to losing their farms to the bank – the bank claimed almost the entire state of Nebraska at that time. To see his children going hungry and his crops dying on the vine brought Raymond's father to tears on more than one occasion, and his father was not a man to show emotions.

The problem today was that Smither's Stream was close to cresting its banks. According to local history, that had never happened before. *God help them all if it did. His neighbors' and his crops would be ruined.*

* * *

The Smith family had lived on their land in central Nebraska for close to 160 years, give or take. Many sections of the farmhouse dated back to its origination; however, his mother insisted on indoor plumbing and a bathroom sometime before his birth in 1953. She said she was tired of getting out of bed at 2:00 A.M. and trekking outside in the weather to sit on the pot whenever nature called. Father once said it made him no mind to go outdoors and relieve himself, but to make Mother happy, he gave in to her request ... *demand.* With some reluctance from his father, a bathroom was added to the farmhouse in the spring of 1950.

The sitting room was original to the home, as far as he knew. It was a small, snug room with a huge, stone fireplace. A flintlock rifle, two deer heads, and elk antlers were mounted above the mantel; a bearskin rug laid on the floor in front of the great hearth. Built-in bookshelves framing it all together were the only changes made to the room that he was aware of. It was his favorite place in the farmhouse; it was his study ... where he went to think and find answers.

He was there now. Rain was falling softly outside when his wife, Ruth, walked into the room and sat down next to him. She knew from the look on her husband's face that he was deeply troubled. Gently taking his hands in hers, she said, 'It's going to be all right, Ray. It's not raining that hard.'

* * *

Married for fifty-three damn-good years, God had blessed them with five children: Samuel, David, Elizabeth Anne, Catherine Anne, and Thomas. David was only three-days old when the Lord called him home to Heaven. Ruth didn't speak a word for five weeks after his death. She just lay in bed, staring at the ceiling and clutching her rosary beads. When she finally spoke, she said the Lord, Our Father, told her it was His will to bring David home to Heaven. David was buried near the rear of the farmhouse in the family graveyard with seven generations of Smiths, and Ruth never spoke his name again except in prayer. Their remaining four children blessed them with eleven grandchildren.

All four of them had moved away, as children raised on a farm tend to do. Samuel moved to New York to live in the *Big Apple*. He worked on Wall Street, trading stocks and bonds. Raymond didn't understand any of that, but his son was happy and making lots of money, living in a big, fancy house with a four-car garage.

Four cars? Why in the world did anyone need four cars when you can only drive one at a time?

Samuel had offered to buy him a new truck, but Raymond refused politely – his old, trusty Ford pickup was enough for him. 'Buy your mother something special if you've a mind to,' Raymond told him. Mother ended up with a new refrigerator and stove, which suited her just fine.

Elizabeth Anne and her husband, Alex, moved with their five children to California some years ago. Alex had the acting bug, and Raymond admitted the boy was good at it. California was the place to be, it seemed, but he and Ruth hated the idea of their grandchildren living so far away.

Catherine Anne and her husband, George, had three sets of twins. *God bless them.* She moved back to the farm from Rhode Island after her husband strayed. The church called men like him *philanderers*. Raymond had his own choice words but kept them to himself. Apparently, George was unable to cope with so many loud children being underfoot and took up with some waitress – never to be heard from again. Raymond had never liked George, even from day one. He thought George had shifty eyes, especially when a pretty skirt was nearby. It was no surprise to Raymond when he took off for parts unknown without so much of a goodbye or a single child support check.

Thomas joined the Marine Corps fresh out of high school. He said he was tired of farm life and wanted to spread his wings ... *see the world.* The first stop on his world tour was Parris Island, South Carolina. Raymond and Ruth journeyed east to see him graduate first in his platoon, wearing his dress blues with a single PFC stripe on his sleeves. Thomas was now in his fourth year of service with two more stripes to show for it and stationed in Okinawa, Japan, of all places. 'Trying to make a career of it ... a thirty-year man,' he said.

* * *

The rain was falling harder, pushing Smither's Stream beyond its brink. Ruth kissed her husband's hand before she stood and walked over to the single window in the study. Raymond had dozed off for a few minutes when the sound of his wife's voice startled him.

'Raymond, you better come to the window and see this!'

In all their years together, he had never heard her voice quake like that, and it sent a chill down his spine. Rising from his chair, he walked over to his wife by the window. Taking her trembling hand in his, he looked out into the storm. The heavy rain made it hard for his old eyes to focus, but then it was there – a twister ... less than two miles away, by his reckoning. It was no ordinary twister, either. It was a monster: over a couple miles wide and moving slowly back and forth, like it was trying to determine which direction it wanted to go.

Ruth's eyes were wide with horror, and her voice quivered when she said, 'Raymond, do we have a chance?'

'Get Catherine Anne and the children down into the fruit cellar!' His voice was hoarse with emotion.

'Will it be enough?' she wondered aloud.

He looked deeply into her brown eyes. *God, how he loved this woman.* He had never lied to his wife before, not once in their fifty-three years, but he lied to her now. 'Yes, honey. The fruit cellar is plenty deep, and we've had more than our fair share of twisters before. Besides, this one looks to be moving toward the east, away from us and the town. Hurry! Do as I ask and get everyone down below. Try not to scare the grandchildren.'

They shared one last look before she hurried off.

She knows I lied. She knows me too well. God help them.

He looked back out into the darkness and saw the monster had chosen it's fated direction.

God help them.

TWO

FEDERAL EMERGENCY MANAGEMENT AGENCY, WASHINGTON, D.C.

April 10, 2030.

Deputy Administrator George Adams sat at his antique, solid-oak rolltop desk and massaged his temples with his fingertips. The looming headache was going to be a whopper, and he was doubtful any amount of aspirin or caffeine would quell it. Looking around his office, his eyes rested upon the clock hanging above the portraits of his two favorite presidents: George Washington standing tall and brave while crossing the icy Delaware River in the dead of winter; Abraham Lincoln sitting in his office with his chin resting on his hand, eyes reflecting the depth of his thoughts. How he wished for the wisdom of these two giants of American history.

The time was 1407 hours. His meeting with Administrator Douglas Wright was scheduled for 1500 hours; fifty-three more minutes until his ass was on the hot seat. He had rerouted Governor Douglas Ryan's report of the storm's damage and projected death toll to his own office before his boss saw it. Three days ago, the tornado in Nebraska had shocked everyone, and he was being called on the carpet to explain why it had not been accurately predicted. The administrator was getting up there in years; his seventy-fifth birthday was only two short months away. To be truthful, many felt he was too old and frail for the stressors and demands of running the Federal Emergency Management Agency (FEMA), but no one dared to mention it. Given that Administrator Wright was a close friend of the president, things were not likely to change any time soon.

Governor Ryan's report was concise, as to be expected from a Harvard Law School graduate. After an extensive, around-the-clock search by local and state law enforcement and the Army National Guard, the early death-toll count stood at 793 based upon the bodies recovered. The most recent census taken prior to the storm listed the population of Broken Bow at 1,107 persons, leaving 314 persons missing. Governor Ryan's report stated no survivors had been located, but the search would continue until all residents were accounted for. Cooperstown and surrounding counties were completely destroyed. The report from FEMA's Regional Office VII (covering Iowa, Kansas, Missouri, and Nebraska) stated the same; however, there was one glaring omission from the governor's report: there had been no storm warning sounded to alert the residents of imminent danger. *Odd for a Harvard man to omit such a pertinent fact from his report. Was Governor Ryan covering his own ass, or did he not know about the lack of a warning?* FEMA, of course, monitored and recorded all emergency early-warning signals throughout the United States. It was no surprise the lack of a storm warning was noted in the FEMA report. It was unheard of in this decade for an immense storm to form and strike without warning. His mouth went dry; if it happened once, though, it most assuredly could happen again.

A knocking at his office door broke his preoccupation with the report. Glancing up, he saw Mrs. Samuels, the secretary for Administrator Wright, standing outside his office door. The worried look in her eyes did not detract from her beautiful yet all-too-serious visage or those shapely legs. He waved for her to enter.

'Hello, Gloria. How are you today? You really should smile more, you know.'

Today's not a day for smiling, Mr. Adams,' she replied.

'Gloria, I've told you many times to call me 'George'. After all, I use your first name, and we have worked together for nearly eight years.'

'Yes, sir, Mr. Adams.'

'That's more like it, *Gloria*,' he replied sarcastically. *She was really too uptight*, he thought. 'What do I owe the pleasure of your company?'

'Well, sir. I called your phone for several minutes with no response.'

'I'm sorry. I had the phone on mute – I needed some quiet time to think. What is it you wanted to discuss? Perhaps lunch at a secluded restaurant or a rendezvous in the coat closet?'

'Mr. Adams, I am a married woman, as you are very well aware.'

'Well, one can hope, can't he? Never mind. Why were you calling?'

'Sir, Administrator Wright wants to see you in his office right away.'

He glanced at his watch. 'It's only 1430 hours. My meeting isn't scheduled for another 30 minutes.'

'Now, sir. But before you head upstairs, fix your tie and comb what's left of your hair.' With that parting shot, she spun on her heels and marched out of his office without a backward glance.

He enjoyed watching her walk away. George sat at his desk a few more minutes, contemplating his decision for leaving his high-paying private-sector position for this one. With a shake of his head, he stood up and walked over to his closet to follow Mrs. Samuels' instructions. Ruefully, he reflected on the full head of hair he had eight years ago when he first began working for FEMA. Sighing, he turned back to his desk and gathered his reports. He wondered if he would still have a job in an hour.

The door leading into Administrator Wright's top-floor office could not have been more different than his own. While his was standard glass and stainless steel of average height, the administrator's door was ten feet of solid mahogany, making a formidable impression on all those who passed through it.

Tax dollars at work, he thought, as Mrs. Samuels opened the door from the inside before he had the opportunity to knock.

'Please come in, Mr. Adams,' she said coyly. She stepped aside to leave as Administrator Wright motioned him into his vast chamber.

'Come in, Mr. Adams, and take a seat.' He pointed to one of the two large leather sofas flanking his desk.

'Yes, sir. Thank you, sir.'

'I'll get straight to the point, Adams. It has come to my attention that the reports from Governor Ryan and Regional Office VII have arrived, but per your instruction, were delivered to your office prior to my viewing them. Is this correct?'

'Yes, sir. I have both with me, sir.'

'That's not exactly standard operating procedure. Is it, Mr. Adams?'

'No, sir. It's not.'

Everyone else on the planet says SOP, Adams thought dryly, but not here behind the ten-foot solid mahogany doors. Was it his imagination or had he just heard Mrs. Samuels snickering behind those same doors? Mrs. Samuels never snickered in her life. She really needed to learn to relax.

The administrator's voice brought him back to the current situation. 'Well, let's have it, Adams. What's your explanation for not following my directive this time … my very clear directive, I might add?'

'Sir, I thought I should read the reports first, so I could brief you on them, myself. The reports from both the governor and the regional office are very upsetting, to say the least. With all the doctor's visits you've had lately – you know your heart condition is common knowledge, after all – I wanted to spare you as much trouble as possible, sir.'

Administrator Wright was silent for a moment and then replied softly, 'That is very kind of you, Mr. Adams. Very kind, indeed.' Then like a switch was flipped, his jaw clenched, and his voice changed. 'But, I am not some child who needs to be coddled or some doddering old fool who needs your protection! Do I make myself clear?' His face was red with anger.

'Yes, sir,' the deputy administrator answered quietly.

Shouting, Wright said, 'LET ME HEAR YOU SAY IT, MR. ADAMS!'

With contrition, Adams said, 'Yes, sir. You've made yourself quite clear, sir.'

Wright calmed down. 'Very good. Now, let's see those reports.'

'Yes, sir.' Adams leaned out to hand the reports to the him, but Wright didn't take them.

The administrator tugged at his goatee and looked upward with deep sadness in his eyes. 'Please lay the reports on my desk in front of me, George.'

It was very rare for him to refer to anyone in the office by his first name, *very rare*. There were only two occasions when he had used George's first name: both times were office parties ... a Christmas party and a retirement party. He noticed Wright was sitting in his wheelchair. He used his wheelchair as scarcely as he did first names; he hated the mobile seat because it made him appear weak and helpless. He believed a man in his position needed to look strong and in complete control.

He must have been in bad shape to concede to the wheelchair. It wasn't a good time for him to be reading two reports listing the current death toll near 800 with the final total possibly reaching more than 1100. Those casualty numbers had already made it the deadliest tornado in U.S. history, slightly ahead of the Tri-State Tornado of 1925.

Despite his abruptness and abrasive personality, everyone at FEMA and all those he worked with knew Administrator Wright's workplace behavior was all an act to hide his embarrassment regarding his disabilities. All those who crossed paths with him, including Adams, were filled with love, respect, and admiration for him. The man was a true hero in every sense of the word. During his military service, he was awarded the Distinguished Service Cross and the Silver Star. His heroic actions while serving as a combat infantry officer with the Army Rangers in Afghanistan were the things they made movies about. He gained even wider respect during his tenure as a very conservative Republican senator and for his time as National Security Advisor under President

Walter Mitchell. Now, he was in charge of FEMA under President Henry R. Holder. His entire life had been devoted to serving his country and countrymen.

As Adams lay the binders within easy reach of Wright, he thought about how deeply the reports were going to impact him. Watching the administrator's face as he slowly processed every page was not easy. His boss's eyes moistened with tears, and the lines around his eyes and mouth deepened.

After several minutes of silent reading, he wiped his eyes and looked up. With an unsteady voice, he said, 'My God ... 793 dead with a very real possibility of no survivors at all. Ghastly.'

Adams responded, 'We don't know that yet, sir. It's still early in the search.'

The administrator shook his head. 'At this point, George, after three solid days of searching, I think it is safe to assume if there are any survivors, the number will be very small.'

Adams broke the uncomfortable silence. 'Sir, would you like me to arrange a meeting at the White House, or do you want to make the call?' Wright seemed to be in a deep trance and not hearing anything being said. Adams walked over to the administrator's side and gently placed his hand on his shoulder. 'Sir? Are you, all right?'

Wright flinched at his touch. 'Yes, George. I'm fine. The president will have to be personally briefed at once. Please make the arrangements ASAP.' He paused. 'Better yet. Have Mrs. Samuels place the call. She knows the protocol better than you do.'

A soft knock at the door interrupted any further discussion. Mrs. Samuels stepped into the doorway.

'Gloria, the deputy administrator and I were just discussing something I need you to do. Please call the White House and arrange for a Priority One meeting with President Holder.'

Uncharacteristically, Gloria Samuels could not make eye contact with Wright. 'Sir, there is a call from your son, Joseph, on line seven.'

The administrator's voice lit up. 'My word! Joseph? I haven't heard from that boy in almost two weeks!' Wright pressed the speakerphone button.

George smirked and silently mouthed to Gloria, 'How's the storm chaser doing?'

Gloria whispered, 'Don't joke, Mr. Adams. Something is very wrong.'

Joseph! How are you, son?'

'Dad? Dad?' (static interrupted his voice)

'Joseph, son. What's wrong? What is it?'

'Dad, I'm in Kansas with my team. I've never … (static) … anything like it. Appeared (static) nowhere!'

'Joseph, what is it? What are you talking about?'

(static) 'A tornado, Dad. It's enormous! … (static) … Dad! Are you there? Answer (static) … me.'

'Where exactly are you, Joe?' Wright's voice was shaking.

(static) Beaver Creek, Dad. We (static) fishing, Dad. No warning … nothing!'

'Son, get away from it! Get your team out of there!'

(static) '… time, Dad. Moving right toward us. Too (static) fast.'

With a loud squeal, the phone went dead. In the deafening silence, Douglas Wright sat very still, his hands gripping the rims of his wheelchair. When he finally spoke, his voice was filled with emotion. 'George, if you would be so kind. Please bring up the satellite screens showing the Beaver Creek region of Kansas.'

'Yes, sir.' With the push of a button, two huge bookcases slid apart, revealing state-of-the-art monitors linked to the National Weather Service (NWS) and the National Oceanic and Atmospheric Administration (NOAA). As the deputy administrator typed in the commands, the screens lit up. 'It's coming online, sir.'

The image displayed was horrific. A line of tornadoes stretched for miles and had all the markings of a super outbreak. By George's rough estimate, he counted at least twenty-seven individual twisters, some very large in size; however, two of them dwarfed the others. Those two were at least three miles wide, which was absolutely unheard of.

George spun around when he heard a thump and gasp of alarm from Mrs. Samuels. Administrator Wright had collapsed in his wheelchair.

THREE

WASHINGTON, D.C.

April 18, 2030.

George Adams awoke to the sound of rain falling. The previous night had been a bad one, filled with nightmares of raging storms and dead friends. He was going to need help to get through the day; he turned on his table lamp next to his bed, grabbed his shot glass, and reached for his closest friend – a bottle of scotch whiskey.

Time to start the day.

The whiskey burned his throat as it slid into his empty stomach, accepting the abuse as it had done the past several mornings. Staggering to the toilet to relieve himself, he cursed the mess he made when he missed. With some shame, he stood before his mirror. The face looking back at him was blotched and swollen, his eyes rimmed red from too many visits with the bottle the night before. 'Only the weak turn to liquor in their time of need,' his sweet mother had been fond of saying. She knew better than anyone; Dad had been an abusive drunk. He was feeling sorry for himself, and truth be told, he was a weak man frightened by too much on his work plate. Who could blame him for needing a pick-me-up from time-to-time, especially this morning.

Nothing like a hot shower, breakfast, and a big cup of coffee, followed by minty-fresh breath to rejuvenate the day. No problem I can't face.

But my God, what a day was in front of him. A horrible, miserable day. First on the agenda for the day was Douglas Wright's funeral followed by an appointment at the White House. The president of the United States of America wanted answers from the new head of FEMA.

* * *

The funeral for Administrator Wright had been delayed by eight days at the request of his widow to allow the rescue teams to find their son's body. Mildred wanted Douglas and Joseph to be buried together, but that would never happen.

Joseph and his fellow storm chasers: John Dyson, Mac Stevens, Billy Watson, and Josh 'Chip' McDonald were all missing. Best friends since their college days at the University of Maryland, storm chasing was their passion, even though they were well into their 40s. Their two camper trucks had been found, but according to classified reports, they were hardly recognizable as vehicles – crushed completely flat like recycling metal at a junkyard.

The entire countryside had been laid to waste. A trailer park of thirty-seven trailers had vanished, leaving only four or five cement bases where the trailers had once stood. A television set with the glass still intact had been found.

How was that even possible?

Some clothing, odds and ends, and a child's teddy bear with a missing eye were found.

Why was the missing eye of the teddy bear included in the report?

The image of the teddy bear and its missing eye kept replaying in his mind until another shot of whiskey was brought to his lips. This time his stomach refused the delivery, and he barely made it to the toilet in time.

Disgusting. Why did he insist on drinking on an empty stomach?

According to the Regional Office VII's report, the Beaver Creek, Kansas, storm held the same F5 classification of the

April 7th storm in Nebraska. F5 tornadoes in two states within three days of each other.

Impossible.

Yet, it happened. The wind speeds of the Kansas twister were measured at more than 307 miles per hour. The recorded rainfall was fifteen inches in less than an hour with hail measuring 4.7 inches in diameter: the largest super-cell tornado in recorded history.

Damn.

The report stated a row of oak trees known to have been rooted for over 180 years were swept away. And the death toll. *Let's not forget the death toll. My God.* Already, 2027 bodies had been recovered in Kansas alone: men, women, and children. The death toll was a new record. The deadliest tornado in world history was the Daulatpur-Saturia tornado in Bangladesh on April 26, 1989, with approximately 1300 dead. Kansas now held the title.

Quiz show contestants have an easier answer to the question for worst tornado in world history for 20 points: Kansas.

A disquieting feeling that these two storms were just the beginning wrenched his gut. Reports of violent storm activity were coming into FEMA from all parts of the globe. There were only a few, but it was enough to know something very wrong was happening. The image of the teddy bear with the missing eye floated through his mind.

* * *

At the end of the funeral for Douglas Wright, a Secret Service agent found George milling around the crowd of mourners. 'Excuse me, Administrator Adams.'

'Yes. What can I do for you?'

'The president wishes to see you at the White House, immediately.'

The man standing before him was clearly Secret Service: three-piece dark suit, a tall and handsome 30-something-year-old with a high-and-tight haircut clean enough to make any Marine drill instructor proud. A rather large bulge under his left arm that was clearly meant to intimidate worked perfectly on George. 'I'm sorry. Who are you, please?' he asked somewhat boldly.

'My name is Special Agent Miller, sir. Secret Service assigned to the presidential detail.'

'Well, Agent Miller. Please inform the president that I have to return to my office to collect my reports.'

'I'm sorry, sir.' With a slight touch to George's sleeve, Agent Miller made it very clear that he was not returning to his office before seeing the president. 'Immediately, sir. As in, *right now.*'

'Of course, Agent Miller. Of course. I'll leave for the White House this moment.'

'Very good, sir,' Agent Miller replied with a tight smile. 'I was hoping you would see things my way.'

* * *

George had the reports in his limousine, and his attempt at stalling was futile. During his eight-year tenure at FEMA, he was privileged to visit the White House twelve times with Administrator Wright. This was his thirteenth – *unlucky thirteenth.* The White House never failed to impress him: the history and the presidents. Today, he was on his own, about to stand in front of the president as the new administrator of FEMA.

* * *

As the driver eased the government limousine up to the rear gate of the White House, George noticed the trees along Pennsylvania Avenue were beginning to bloom with apple blossoms. The arrival of spring did very little to lift his sour mood. A steady rain was falling, and the windshield wipers were making an unpleasant squelching noise that put George's teeth on edge.

Unconsciously, George reached into the pocket of his vest for his flask. It wasn't there, of course; he had left it on his bed, tucked under his pillow, awaiting his return.

The limousine driver slowed the car to a stop for the Marine sentry's mandatory identification check and was waved through.

No backing out.

He exited the limo, only to be greeted by an aide with an umbrella. *VIP treatment at its best*, he thought. *I could get used to this.* Unfortunately, VIP treatment came with a high cost under the current administration. It was well-known throughout Washington D.C., that the president was a harsh taskmaster who was intolerant of mistakes. He easily dismissed subordinates if he found them remotely inadequate. He was a fair man but tough. President Henry R. Holder wanted to be remembered in history as one of the all-time greatest presidents, and he was relentless to achieve it.

George was escorted to a conference room adjoining the Oval Office. From his time spent here with Administrator Wright, he knew the excessively large, dark-plush carpeted room was magnificent and meant to create a lasting impression with its nineteenth-century, Virginian clawfoot conference table flanked by fourteen chairs and walls lined with historical battle scenes spanning from the Revolutionary War to the Korean War. He entered the room, and four heads turned to face him. President Holder sat at the head of the table, as expected, with Vice President William B. Timmons to his left. Neither appeared pleased to see him or to be sitting next to each other. The men loathed each other and only joined forces after a dirty campaign to combine efforts to keep the other party out of office. On the president's right was his longtime secretary, Abigail Fitzgerald. She was a stout, grey-haired, sixty-year-old woman who always wore her hair in a bun as tight as her grimace. Ms. Fitzgerald looked at George as if he were something unpleasant stuck to the bottom of her shoe. To Ms. Fitzgerald's right sat National Security Advisor William O'Henry, a lifelong politician and the only one who smiled.

President Holder spoke in his east Texas drawl, 'I am sorry I sent the Secret Service for you at Administrator Wright's funeral, Mr. Adams, but you left me no choice in the matter. Ms. Fitzgerald placed several calls to both your office and your home with no response. Would you care to explain?' Ms. Fitzgerald was glaring at him.

My apologies, sir. I've not been feeling well. My office was aware that I was home, sick in bed.'

'Yes, Mr. Adams. Your office made your situation known to Ms. Fitzgerald. What I would like to know is whether you were ill or simply intoxicated.'

'Sir?'

'Come now, Mr. Adams. The question is an easy one,' challenged the president. 'I know you have a problem with alcohol. There are very few secrets in Washington. Administrator Wright may have tolerated your behavior in the past, or perhaps looked the other direction concerning your indiscretions, but I will not. You're allowed only one mistake in my administration ... one. I hope for your sake that I have made myself quite clear on this point.'

'Yes, sir. Very clear,' stammered George.

'Let me explain something to you,' continued the president. 'The reason you are the administrator of FEMA is due to a promise I made to Douglas. He was like a brother to me, and when his heart condition worsened, he asked me as a personal favor to appoint you as his replacement in the event of his death. You must understand, Mr. Adams. Douglas was very fond of you.'

George Adams took a deep breath to compose himself and said, 'Thank you, Mr. President. I was very fond of Administrator Wright, too.'

President Holder cleared his throat and stated, 'I know how you felt about him, George, but I must make you aware that your appointment may not be a permanent one. Any permanency will be based on your overall job performance, and more importantly, your desire to stay sober. Please take a seat next to Vice President Timmons and let us proceed with our meeting.' The president adjusted his seat and appeared uncharacteristically uncertain as to how to continue. With a sigh, he removed his glasses and rubbed the bridge of his nose. 'The first question I need to ask you, George, is have the bodies of Joseph and his companions been located yet?'

'No, sir. None of the five men have been recovered.'

'In your opinion, will they ever be located?'

'I don't believe so, sir. We know the approximate location of their campsite based on Joseph's final phone call and from where we found the two camper trucks they were using, but nothing else has been recovered in a three-mile search grid conducted by the Army National Guard. I'm very sorry, Mr. President.'

Vice President Timmons interrupted and asked, 'Have you discontinued the search, Mr. Adams? After all, it's been eight days.'

'I am awaiting further instruction on that matter from President Holder, sir.'

'Well, I don't wish to be insensitive to the families of those five young men, but in my opinion, any continued search would be futile,' stated the vice president.

President Holder glared at the vice president before speaking, 'I will be the judge of when to call off the search, William.'

'Of course, Mr. President. I was just stating my opinion on the matter,' grunted Timmons.

'George, I want the search to be continued for another ten days, at the minimum. Please inform the National Guard of my order as soon as this meeting in concluded.'

'Yes, sir, Mr. President.'

'Let's proceed with the matter at hand,' continued President Holder. 'What information can you provide us on these two storms, George?'

George Adams lifted his heavy briefcase from the floor and placed it on top of the conference room table. Unclicking the latches of his case, he removed the burgeoning manila folders holding the data from the storms, including the increasing death tolls. His mouth was dry, and he was desperate for a drink.

Hold it together. You can do this.

The pitcher of water in front of him had to suffice for the moment as he poured himself a full glass and took a sip. 'Well, sir. The information is ghastly, sorry to say. The death toll stands at 1053 bodies recovered from the Nebraska storm. The most recent census conducted for that region reported the population at 1107. That leaves approximately fifty-four individuals unaccounted for. The town and surrounding farms were completely leveled.'

'What was the name of the town, Mr. Adams? I need the information for my meeting minutes,' explained Ms. Fitzgerald.

19

'Cooperstown, Ms. Fitzgerald.' George shifted uneasily in his chair. 'According to FEMA's Regional Office VII, which is responsible for the state of Nebraska, no advance tornado warning was issued.'

Speaking for the first time, National Security Advisor William O'Henry asked, 'How do you account for that?'

'The speed with which the storm formed would be my best guess, sir.' George reached for his glass and spilled a small amount of water on the antique table. No one appeared to notice except for Ms. Fitzgerald who huffed and wiped up the spill with a napkin.

'Isn't it unusual for no warning to be issued, George?'

'Yes, Mr. President. Most unusual. Since I've been associated with FEMA, it has never happened before, and it has occurred twice now in the span of three days.'

Vice President Timmons was surprised. 'There was *no* warning issued for the Kansas storm, either, Mr. Adams?'

'No, sir. Both storms formed and struck without a warning being issued.'

President Holder sat silently in his armchair. His face was grim as he processed the details. His left hand was clenching his ever-present pipe. The slow ticking of the eight-foot tall grandfather clock reverberated throughout the room for several minutes until the president finally spoke in a voice barely above a whisper. 'My God. One thousand fifty-three confirmed dead. No warning given. How is that possible?'

'I'm very sorry to report, sir, but I'm afraid the data is much worse concerning Kansas.'

Abigail Fitzgerald stood up and moved gently to the president's side, touching him slightly on the shoulder. Her eyes were moist, and the depth of their friendship became evident to George. President Holder looked up at Ms. Fitzgerald and placed his hand over hers. 'I'm fine, Abby. Really. Please take your seat and let Mr. Adams continue with his report. Please proceed, George.'

'Yes, sir. As I was saying, the news is much worse for Kansas. The most recent report from the National Guard, confirmed by Regional Office VII, is that the death toll stands at 2027 confirmed dead and approximately 4000 to 5000 still missing. We will not have an exact number on the dead and missing for at least a few weeks, maybe even months.'

Vice President Timmons asked, 'Why is that, Mr. Adams?'

'The path of destruction for the Kansas storm was much larger than that of the Nebraska storm, sir.'

'How much larger?' asked National Security Advisor O'Henry.

'One moment, sir. I have those numbers in a separate file,' replied Adams as he leafed through his folders. 'Ah, here it is. The Nebraska super cell covered an area roughly 11 square miles with its center located over Cooperstown and the surrounding farms. The preliminary study done of the Kansas storm by FEMA and the Army Corps of Engineers states the super cell covered 57 square miles.'

'What damage estimates for the Kansas storm can you provide us with, Mr. Adams?' asked Vice President Timmons.

'That information is in its early stages, sir. For now, the estimation is $275 million. Three small towns along with several trailer parks were completely leveled.'

'Mr. Adams, once again, can you provide the names of the three towns and the exact number you mean when you say *several* trailer parks?' asked Ms. Fitzgerald.

'I'm sorry. Yes, I can. The towns were: Stanford, Beech-Haven, and Long Branch. There were five trailer parks destroyed.'

'Thank you very much, Mr. Adams,' murmured Ms. Fitzgerald.

'I have some small understanding of tornadoes and how they are formed, George,' stated the president. 'As I understand it, there is a grading system used to report how powerful the storm is. Is that true?'

'That is correct, sir.'

'So, what grade was assigned to these two storms or *super cells*, as you have referred to them?'

'If I may, sir, let me clarify. At FEMA, we use the term *classification* instead of *grade*. The answer to your question is they were both classified as F5s.'

Vice President Timmons scowled. 'Is that the highest classification on the scale, Mr. Adams?'

'Yes, sir. It is. The scales range from the lowest point, which is an F1, to the highest, an F5.'

'I have a feeling you are reluctant to share some information with us, George,' challenged President Holder. 'Let's hear it all, please.'

Everyone at the conference table exchanged confused looks except for George Adams.

George stared at the president for several seconds before he licked his lips and replied. 'According to my research, Mr. President, two F5 tornadoes occurring within a span of three days has never happened before. In fact, the odds of a single tornado forming into an F5 are less than 0.1 percent.'

All were stunned into silence until the president finally asked, 'Where do these two storms rank historically, George?'

'The deadliest tornado in world history was on April 26, 1989, in Bangladesh. It destroyed the towns of Manikganj Sadar and Saturia. Approximately 1300 were reported dead with an additional 12,000 injured.'

'Do you have anything more to add before we conclude this meeting, George?' asked President Holder.

'There is one more item, sir. As I am sure you are aware, Europe and Asia have seen some rather disturbing weather patterns in the past week, also. My office has received reports of softball-sized hail in different regions of England and France; yesterday, Japan experienced an earthquake measuring 7.1 on the Richter scale. As of this morning, we have not received any information on a possible death toll or damage from Japan.'

'I am aware of the earthquake in Japan, George, but I had not heard about the hail. I am uncertain if those events relate to our weather problems here in the United States,' stated the president.

'Sir, I believe it's a pattern of global weather change. To be blunt, I strongly believe these storms will not only continue but worsen.'

'What scientific proof do you have to back up such an outlandish statement, Mr. Adams,' scoffed Vice President Timmons.

'None at this time, sir.'

'Then, please confine your remarks to the facts and keep all statements about worsening global weather patterns to yourself. Do I make myself clear, Mr. Adams?'

'Very clear, sir.'

'I agree with the vice president, George, but I want you to consider that as a direct order coming from me. We cannot alarm the worldwide population based on your assumptions.'

'I had no intention of voicing my concerns beyond this room, Mr. President.'

'I'm glad we understand each other. If there is nothing further to report, this meeting is concluded.'

* * *

His bedroom was dark except for the nightlight he had used since childhood. George poured himself another shot of rye and swallowed it whole. His thoughts plagued him and kept his desire for sleep at a distance. He should have told President Holder of his visions, but how?

I have a responsibility and an obligation to humanity to tell what I have seen.

Those four individuals sitting around the conference room table already considered him an alcoholic and quite possibly delusional.

Why add probable cause for a psychological evaluation?

He wasn't insane or delusional. He had seen the storms in Kansas and Nebraska take form and strike days before their arrival; the screams of the dying reverberated inside his head. His visions, or *sights*, had been with him his entire life. His maternal grandmother was blessed – *cursed* – with the *visions*, but she called it her third eye. She asked him at the tender age of eight if he had ever seen things happen before they did or see where misplaced possessions were, and he answered truthfully, 'Yes, Nana. I can do that, but my friends can't. Sometimes, they ask me to help them find their lost toys. I don't think Mommy or Daddy can do it because they aren't able to find anything they've lost.'

His grandmother took him into her arms and hugged him. 'You have a special gift from God, my little George. He has great plans for you – only a few people are blessed with a third eye.'

At eight-years-old, George formed a picture of a creepy third eye smack dab in the middle of his forehead. From that moment forward, he called his gift from God his *sight* until he was an adult. Now, he referred to it as his *vision*.

Pulling his blanket tightly around him, he prayed that the two storms he had envisioned in Nebraska and Kansas were freaks of nature and not to be repeated in his lifetime, but he knew there were many more to come. He poured himself another drink, hoping he might fall asleep quickly; like so many other nights, he was afraid to fall asleep ...

FOUR

VATICAN CITY. ROME, ITALY.

May 3, 2030.

It was an hour or so before sunrise, and St. Peter's Square stood silent and mostly empty except for two young lovers walking hand-in-hand and a few faithful early risers starting their day in prayer and meditation. Soon the square would be filled with tourists taking photographs and small groups milling about, making passageway difficult for one moving as slowly as he did. Father Joseph Camassei with his ever-present cane in one hand and tiny cup of cappuccino in the other always preferred this time of day to walk around the piazza. He enjoyed the peace and quietness: the rare solitude of introspection he treasured as he grew older.

A light overnight rain and low-lying sparse fog made his walk across the ancient cobblestones somewhat cumbersome, but a clean fragrance filled the air. From where he stood, he could see a single candle burning in Father Francis's study window. On the balcony outside of the window, a large garden bloomed: zucchini, lettuce, peppers, and Father Francis's prized tomatoes. Father Joseph stared at the candle for another moment; it was useless to Father Francis, of course, but he enjoyed the smell of burning wax and the small comfort it gave;

however, its real purpose was to summon Father Joseph to his bed chamber.

* * *

Years ago, he had been ordered to appear before Cardinal Angelo Tommaso Borgogni, second only to his Holiness, Pope Nicholas. Apprehension did not adequately describe his feelings when he walked through the ornate office and took his seat before the cardinal. The meeting, considering its importance, had been brief.

'Father Joseph, you have been blessed with the trust of his Holiness, and what I am about to reveal unto you is of the utmost secrecy – never to be discussed with any person. Do you understand?'

'Not completely, Eminence.'

Cardinal Borgogni sat behind his enormous desk and studied Father Joseph for a moment before continuing. 'Within these walls are two prophets of the church. Their names are Sister Adelina Bonomo and Father Francis Fornicola.'

'I have never heard of them, Eminence,' Father Joseph replied flatly.

'No, you would not have, Father Joseph. There is no knowledge of either of them beyond his Holiness, several others whom you need not concern yourself with, and me.'

Father Joseph shifted uncomfortably in his chair. 'May I know the reason for this secrecy, Eminence?'

The cardinal ignored the question as he stood and walked over to the window overlooking Piazza San Pietro. 'You, Father Joseph, have been chosen to be both aide and confidant to Sister Adelina and Father Francis, visiting each of them twice daily. You will take notes, word-for-word, of anything they discuss with you and feed them their meals. Let me make myself crystal clear on the next point. Sister Adelina and Father Francis are very much aware of each other but have never met. Nor will they ever meet. You must never divulge any information to either that the other has said. This is most critical. Do you understand, Father Joseph?'

'I understand, Eminence.'

Cardinal Borgogni returned to his seat and stared deeply into the eyes of the priest sitting across from him. 'Good. I pray for your sake that you do, Father Joseph. Upon conclusion of your meetings with both each day, you will report directly to me with your written statements of every word spoken. In the rare event I am unavailable, you will report to his Holiness and no one else.'

Taken aback by the cardinal's last statement, Father Joseph asked, 'His *Holiness*, Eminence?'

The cardinal breathed a sigh of impatience. 'Yes, Father Joseph, his Holiness. There are several more items we need to discuss before I release you to your new responsibilities. Sister Adelina is somewhat *grotesque* in appearance. I only tell you this, so you are not startled when you first meet her. No one knows exactly how old she is, but she is quite old and frail. In addition, you must never allow yourself to be touched by Sister Adelina or touch her for any reason. Do you understand, Father?'

'I am sorry, Eminence. I do not understand why there is such a request.'

'This is not a request, Father Joseph. This is a command from myself and Pope Nicholas.'

'May I have an explanation, Eminence?'

Cardinal Borgogni bowed his head as if in prayer. With a sigh of despair, he raised his face and stared at the father. 'I am very sorry, Joseph, but I cannot provide you with an answer to your question at this time. Please know that Pope Nicholas and I would not make this demand unless it were of the utmost importance. Please ask no more about it.'

'Of course, Eminence. I will follow your instructions as directed.'

'Thank you, Father Joseph. The last discussion of concern regards Father Francis. He is seventy-nine years old and is blind.'

* * *

The rain began to fall as Father Joseph made his way through Piazza San Pietro. His knees and back protested at the quickening of his pace, but his work day began at the lighting of Father Francis's candle. Reaching the side doorway that led to the residence of Sister Adelina and Father Francis, he was greeted by two of the ten Swiss Guard solders who protected the residence and two very precious individuals of the Vatican, around the clock, seven days per week.

The Swiss Guard greeted him for years in the same manner. 'Good morning, Father Joseph. May we see your passport, please?'

He breathed out a portentous sigh and reached into his overcoat's pocket for his identification papers and pass. No one was permitted to enter the residence without a pass signed and dated by Cardinal Borgogni, except for his Holiness.

As the guard checked his pass, Father Joseph glanced back at the piazza. The sky was dark and ominous; the rain falling harder than before. Streaks of lightning flashed in the distance as his overcoat billowed with the gusts of wind. The piazza was empty except for a lone figure, knelt in prayer before St. Peter's Basilica. He studied the pilgrim who was unfazed by the change in weather. *Faith is a wonderful and beautiful thing to behold*, he thought, as the huge doors slowly closed and locked behind him.

The dark hallway leading to the chamber of Father Francis was plain by Vatican standards – bereft of artwork, frescoes, and furniture – except for a small table outside the doorway of the father's bedchamber, where the food tray was placed at mealtimes. Every breakfast consisted of a plate with three eggs over medium, bacon, thinly sliced ham, toast, coffee, and a large glass of orange juice. Lunch was never served, per his request, but dinner was always pasta with a large salad, two pieces of bread and butter, goat cheese, and a small glass of wine. Two soldiers, standing on either side of the doorway, nodded in their acknowledgment of his arrival. They were forbidden, except in an emergency, to enter either bedchamber, so it was Father Joseph's responsibility to deliver the meals to the father and sister.

Rapping once on the chamber door, he entered without waiting for a response. Father Francis was sitting on a seat by his balcony as he did every morning. His small bed was already made and covered with a heavy quilt; a large crucifix hung above the headboard. Everything in his room was neat and tidy, including the bare wood floor. Father Joseph stopped for a moment to reflect on the fact he had never seen Father Francis in his bed. Whenever he visited him, he was either sitting on his favorite chair or tending to his garden on the balcony.

'Good morning, Francis. How are you on this blessed morning, my brother?'

The father tilted his head and moved his sightless eyes upward to the voice of his friend. 'Joseph, come and stand next to me. Take my hand. How was your morning stroll, my dear friend?'

'Ah, my brother. It rained last evening and continues to do so this morning, as you are well aware. The cobblestones were slippery and walking over them was difficult with my cane, but I enjoyed it as usual. Let me set your breakfast tray down. How was your sleep last night, my friend?'

When no reply was forthcoming, Father Joseph stopped setting up the breakfast table and went to his friend's side. 'What is it, Francis? What troubles you?'

'Joseph, please bring over the stool and sit next to me; I need comforting.'

'Of course. Please tell me what is causing you such distress.'

Sitting quietly and taking a sip of his coffee, Father Francis wore a grave expression. 'My soul is in torment this morning, my brother. I do not have visions daily, as you are aware, but when I do, I can most often interpret what I have seen without any guidance from you or Cardinal Borgogni. This morning is different.'

'How is it different, Francis?'

'Last night, I had the same repeated vision. I would wake from the nightmare only to fall back to sleep and have it return,' whispered Father Francis.

Joseph squeezed his friend's hand. 'What was it you saw, my brother?'

'Before I answer your question, Joseph, let me ask one of you. Do you believe in what I portent?'

'That is a difficult question for me to answer, Francis. Not every vision you have shared with me has come to pass.'

29

'Everything I have told you, every vision ever shared, will come to pass, Joseph. You would do well to have more faith in the power of evil and good, my brother.'

'I am sorry if I have upset you, Francis. It was never my intent to do so. It is just that most of the visions you have shared with me are disturbing, to say the least. One might even call them *apocalyptic* in nature.'

'There is more truth to what you said than you realize, Joseph. No, I am not upset with you or your words but with what I have seen this past night.'

'Will you share your vision with me, Francis?'

'In a moment, Joseph. First, I need some time to rest.'

'Why don't you eat your breakfast before it gets cold? Perhaps you might feel better after you've eaten. You must be hungry.'

'Yes, I am.' Breakfast was eaten in silence, as Father Francis preferred. Not a word was spoken from the end of his prayer of thanksgiving until he finished his last sip of coffee. At last, he sat back in his armchair and reached out for Joseph's hand. 'I will share what I have seen, Joseph, and realize it will surely come to pass in our lifetime.'

I am here for you, Francis. Please share your burden with me.'

There was a long, silent pause – the ticking of the mantel clock and the peaceful melody of the rain falling were the only sounds in the room.

When Father Francis eventually spoke, it was barely above a whisper. 'I never told you how I lost my eyesight, did I?'

'No, you have never shared your story with me.'

'There was no medical reasoning for the loss of my eyesight, even by the finest doctors. I have been a priest for fifty-three of my seventy-nine years, Joseph. The Lord, our Father, took my eyesight when I was but a young man of thirty-two. I am not complaining, mind you. The Lord blessed me with many gifts in return: one being the gift of divination. I kept the gift a secret for many years. In its early stages, I knew things such as what the weather would be like weeks in advance or what someone would tell me in confession. Nothing of much significance. But after some time, the visions grew darker and more disturbing.'

Father Joseph cleared his throat and asked, 'Can you give me an example, Francis?'

Standing up, Father Francis slowly felt his way along the room to his balcony. The rain was coming down in heavy sheets, and the sky was an ugly shade of gray. Lightning flashed in the distance. 'I can give you an example, but it's not a pleasant one to share.'

'Please do.'

'I could *see* when a friend, loved one, or parishioner was about to die.

Father Joseph Camassei sat in stunned silence. 'My God! What did you do with this knowledge?'

'What could I do except pray? I did seek counsel after a time from a dear friend of mine, Bishop Cook. I was able to convince him that I was indeed blessed with divination, and he informed the Vatican immediately. I was brought to Rome at the age of thirty-four and have been locked in this room ever since. Once again, I am not complaining. The Lord provided me with a great gift in which to serve the church and provide warning of the beginning of Revelations.

'Take my hands, Joseph. You must understand that I never wanted to burden you with any of this, but time grows short, and it is my duty to share all that I know.'

'I understand, and I do not consider what visions you have shared with me to be a burden, my brother.'

'That is good to hear. There are seven prophets in all: Sister Adelina, three young men in the United States, a young girl of seven living somewhere in France, a monk living in a monastery in the south of Spain, and me. Their names and exact locations are unknown to me. I believe if I had that information, they, too, would be locked within these very walls. There are moments when I *see* personal things relating to each of my fellow prophets: the young girl's age; the monk's vow of silence to never speak of the visions he receives when he closes his eyes for sleep.'

'Francis, you speak this morning as though you have been held prisoner within these walls. Tell me the truth, my friend. Is that how you feel?'

'Leaving this bedchamber is not allowed, Joseph. Have you never wondered why the Swiss Guard stands a constant watch over me? Regardless of that being said, I do not view myself as a prisoner.'

Father Joseph Camassei felt overwhelmed with sudden trepidation. 'We have known each other for many years, Francis. I have been by your side twice-daily to listen to your visions. Please, Francis, after all these years, why tell me now about your purpose to warn the church of the beginning of Revelations and of the other prophets besides yourself and Sister Adelina? What vision did you have last night to cause you to speak as you have this morning?'

A long silence once again spread throughout the small bedchamber. In a trembling voice, Father Francis Fornicola said, 'The end is near, my brother. The trumpet will sound soon, and the Horsemen will ride forth. The purpose of the seven is to warn humanity to prepare for Judgement Day.' Hesitating for a moment, he took a deep breath and continued, 'In my vision last night, I saw rats, my brother. Rats were feasting on the bones of humanity, and they were smiling.'

* * *

Father Joseph slipped through Father Francis's bedchamber door and closed it softly behind him. One of the soldiers stepped up swiftly and bolted it –the sound echoed down the dark hallway. Hands shaking, his cane-assisted gait was unsteady as he made his way toward Sister Adelina's room. He dreaded his time with her, but today's visit seemed to loom over him. If his close friend could make him feel as ill as he did at this moment, what were his expectations with Sister Adelina? Picking up her breakfast tray, he waited as the Swiss Guard unlocked her door. Knocking gently to announce his presence, her rasping voice answered, 'Please come in, Father Joseph.'

Entering her bedchamber, a feeling of dread he had never experienced before washed over him. The room was pitch black, save for a dim candle burning near her bedside, casting ghost-like shadows on the walls. 'Good morning, Sister Adelina. How are you feeling today?' There was no answer. He placed her breakfast tray on the table next to her and noticed he could barely discern her slight form under the blankets. Her breathing was laborious, and the smell in the room was as pungent as always. 'What shall we discuss this morning, Sister Adelina?' Again, no answer ... which was not all that unusual. Sister Adelina rarely had anything to say, and he was thankful for it now because it meant less time in her presence. As he prepared to leave the room, he said, 'I'll be back this evening with your dinner, Sister Adelina. Enjoy your breakfast. Good day to you.'

As he reached for the doorknob, Sister Adelina murmured, 'Father Joseph, I have something to ask of you.'

Turning with trepidation, Father Joseph stared at the diminutive figure sitting up in her bed. 'Yes, Sister? What is it you wish to know?'

With a voice that would haunt his dreams every night from that moment on, she asked, 'Did Father Francis tell you about the rats?'

FIVE

CENTRAL PARK, NEW YORK CITY, NEW YORK.

May 21, 2030.

It was a rare day in New York City; the sky was a clear shade of blue, and the air smelled fresh. It appeared the air's pollution had taken a day's vacation. Even the pollen count seemed to be down. Some folks called New York City the *concrete jungle*. Robert Gray believed he knew the truth in that statement better than most people, as he plodded his way toward Central Park with his chessboard tucked underneath his beefy arm.

New York was a jungle, and it was about to get a whole lot worse … *very soon*. Last night's dream sent a shudder down his large spine. People were about to get a wake-up call, a very ugly, very unpleasant wake-up call; he couldn't think of a worse place to be than New York City when it happened, but where else was he to go? New York, after all, was his home. He felt out of place anywhere else and had spent his entire life on these streets. Besides, what was coming down the road was going to affect the entire human population.

Affect? That was an odd word for him to have used with the human race facing extinction, or annihilation, or a horrible, agonizing end. Stop it! Stop thinking about it.

There was nothing he could do … nothing anyone could do. The end was near, and there would be no survivors. No place for anyone to hide. Perhaps it was time for the slate to be cleaned, and God had finally acknowledged what a fucked-up mistake it had all been.

Passing a basketball court, he sensed the sudden movement toward him before seeing it. Two local gang members of *The Bloods* who had laid claim to this particular block approached him before they got a good look at their prospective prey. The twenty-six-year veteran of the N.Y.P.D. stood six feet seven inches tall and weighed in at a solid 290 pounds. None of it was donut fat, either. With eighteen-inch biceps that most gym rats would envy, he was a powerful man in both appearance and manner … he was not someone to mess with. He rarely spoke, and his ruddy face almost never smiled.

Once, on a dare, a tough-looking biker had asked him at the local bar why he never spoke to anyone. 'You too good to talk with us, man?' Without a word, Gray dropped the biker with one punch, breaking his jaw in three places. Gray went back to his beer and whiskey chaser without a backward glance. No one in the pub ever spoke to him again after that night, which was just the way Robert Gray liked for things to be.

The two gang members stopped in their tracks and stared up at him. It was quite obvious from their demeanor that they wanted no part of this hulking white man standing in front of them. Their so-called *pride* was at stake, and neither of them wanted to be the first to back down.

Gray took matters into his own very large hands. 'Look, guys. I don't want any trouble with you, and it's very clear neither of you want any trouble with me. Let's just call it a draw, and we'll each go our separate way. Is that cool with you?'

'Sure, man. No problem. We don't want no hassle.' The two Blood members sauntered off, down the dirty sidewalk with their hands deep in their pockets, on the lookout for an easier mark. Gray reflected for a moment: he should have let them make their move and even antagonized them a bit instead of talking them out of it. He was an officer of the law, after all, but it would have felt good and even lifted his spirits to break both their heads wide open and run them in. *Next time. There's always a next time.* Besides, he was late for his chess game.

Central Park was springing to life; he slowed his pace to enjoy the moment. The cherry blossoms and red oak trees were in full bloom, and wildflowers were everywhere he looked. Not many people thought a man such as he could enjoy nature, but he did. He knew his closest friend, Albert Walker (his only friend, for that matter, apart from his cat, Cotton), would be waiting for him at their usual park bench, ready to play their daily game of chess or checkers. Al would understand his dreams. They had been partners for most of his twenty-six years on the police force and walked a beat together more miles than either of them cared to remember; saved each other's ass on more than a few occasions, too. Except for that one day ...

***

The memory stopped him in his tracks, and the beautiful May morning faded from his view into a tunnel of darkness. Al had been sick that day ... several days, in fact. Hell, most of the department had the flu that week, so manpower had been minimal. Most officers worked without a partner during that time period, and he had been one of them. March 18th had been a cold afternoon, and it was a few minutes past four o'clock, meaning his shift was almost over. Gray could not say for sure what had made him go into that store. It was just one of those average run-of-the-mill check-cashing establishments. Nothing special about it, and no reason for him to go inside the business; however, he walked inside only to have a gun pointed at him within three feet of his forehead and a second gun's barrel pressed into his back. *Rock and a hard place, for damned sure.* Armed robbery in progress, and like an idiot, he had walked right into it.

The two assailants took him into a rear storage room, threw him to the floor facedown, and tied his wrists to his ankles: hogtied, nice and tight. They took his service weapon and then started the rough stuff. They kicked and punched him a few times for the fun of it, he guessed. They stood off to the side, debating whether they should let him live or put a bullet into the back of his head. When they finally left, the shame set in and set in for good, taking up permanent residency in his memory, you might say. He had given up without any fight at all. As the years went by, the nightmares had lessened, but the shame he carried, *still carried*, never went away. Even his own brother had asked him, 'Why didn't you pull your gun?' If his own brother had questioned about his actions that day *or rather his inactions*, what must members of his own department be thinking? *I should have pulled my gun*, he thought for the thousandth time. *I should have pulled my gun. It would have been much better to have died at that moment. A man should not have to live with shame all his life.*

***

'Are you going to stand in the sun all day, staring at those big feet of yours, or are we going to play some chess? Hey, Rob. Do you hear me? Rob?'

Robert Gray tilted his head up. He had been so lost in thought that Al had been able to approach him without his knowledge. *Not good.* Ever since that March day, Gray had prided himself on being more aware of his surroundings. 'Yeah, I'm fine, Al. Just stopped to think for a second.'

'A second? I've been watching you stand like a statue for close to five minutes and have been talking to you for at least a minute with no response. You sure you're okay?'

'Yeah, buddy. I said I'm fine. Drop the fucking subject, okay?' He immediately regretted snapping at his friend. 'Sorry, Al. I just had a run-in with two punks. I didn't mean to bite your head off.'

'No problem, big guy. What happened?'

'Not much, Al. Two hoods made the mistake of thinking they had an easy mark. I changed their minds for them.'

'Did you have to break some heads to do it?'

'No, nothing like that. Just words back and forth. No big deal. Let's play some chess; I feel like beating your ass on the board.'

'Fine, but I have to warn you ... I've learned some new moves since we last played.'

'You need some new moves, Al. Beating you in chess or checkers hardly feels special anymore.'

* * *

'What was that about beating me? I've won two games in a row. It's like you're not even trying. You sure that you're all right?'

'Sorry, Al. I guess my mind's not on the game today. Or those new chess moves of yours have me completely befuddled.'

'It's all good, man. I have to be going soon, anyway. I promised my new lady-friend I'd have lunch with her and take her shopping afterward.'

'Shopping? You're taking her shopping? What's come over you, Al? Is this thing between you two getting serious?'

'Yeah. I really like this one. She makes a mean peanut butter and jelly sandwich. You should try meeting someone one of these days. It would get you out of the closet you call an apartment and away from your mangy cat.'

'I don't think any woman would find me to be good company. And I've told you many times in the past not to call Cotton *mangy*.'

'Don't sell yourself short, Rob. You have a lot to offer to the right person. I'll see you tomorrow, buddy. Same time, same place?'

'Sure, Al. Tomorrow. Have lots of fun *shopping*.'

* * *

Arriving back at his apartment, Gray put his chess game away in the hallway closet and went to the refrigerator to make himself some lunch. He methodically piled pepperoni, anchovies, and two slices of Swiss cheese between two thick slices of Italian bread slathered with mayonnaise and grabbed a beer. For dessert … a large piece of chocolate cake. *A perfect meal.*

As he plunked himself into his favorite chair to watch the ballgame, Cotton stretched and curled around his master's feet. He was looking for a handout, no doubt. Gray fed the cat some small bites of anchovies and settled back into his chair to think things out.

Although by appearances one might think he was a religious man, he was not. Far from it, as a matter of fact. Sure, he attended church on a regular basis, but he also made his appearances in synagogues and other places of worship several times per week. His reasons were not spiritual ones; he was searching for answers to the many questions plaguing his thoughts. *Why? Why am I alive? Why is anyone alive for that matter?* Life, to his way of thinking, was a huge waste of time. Feeling contemplative, he took a long sip of his beer. *From the moment you are born, the angel of death has you marked with an expiration date stamped on your damn forehead. Your life could well end with either your very first breath or one hundred years from that moment. Regardless, your life will end: one hundred years or not, what had been the point of it all?* The one question that troubled him the most and kept him awake late at night: why had he been cursed with these damned visions of the apocalypse? *Why me, of all people?*

* * *

Rising slowly from his chair, Gray went into the bathroom. He stared at his reflection in the cracked mirror for a long time. Opening his medicine cabinet, he grabbed the pills he had hidden in a container of bandages on the top shelf. Inside the pills was Nembutal, a very powerful poison he had obtained while on vacation in Mexico three years ago. Suicide was a grave sin, even noted as an unforgivable sin in the church sectors. Although he was not a religious man, he knew that Hell existed. He had seen it many times in his nightmares. If Hell existed, then Heaven must also. Cotton sauntered into the bathroom, jumped onto the side of the sink, and sat on his haunches ... purring and staring up at his friend in a reproachful manner. Gray shelved the pills and closed the cabinet. 'Not today,' he said aloud. Besides, he had promised Al that they would play chess tomorrow. Feeling the weight of the world on his shoulders, Gray changed into his shabby robe and gently picked up his cat. Lying down on his bed, he held his purring companion tightly to his chest and silently cried himself to sleep.

SIX

YELLOWSTONE NATIONAL PARK, WYOMING.

May 31, 2030.

An unusually cold breeze softly blew the cabin's curtains apart and woke him long before his alarm clock had been set to go off. He surveyed the interior of the large, log cabin he shared with nine other park rangers. No one else stirred. For the moment, he had the morning to himself. Ethan R. Hardy, shivering from the cold, swung his long legs off his bed, stood, and walked to the huge black, cast-iron stove to heat the water for coffee. One of his fellow rangers turned in his sleep, mumbled the name 'Diane,' and then went back to snoring. Outside, Ethan could hear the wind picking up speed. He went to the window and peered out. In the dimness, he could see the beginning light of the morning sky. It appeared to be mostly clear with a few clouds off to the west. At worst, there might be a light shower. He hoped for the best because today was the first day of his new assignment. If it rained too hard, he would have to go back to the drudgery of the despised gatehouse. He knew all rookie park rangers had to do their time working inside the gatehouse. After all, important questions from the incoming campers and tourists pertaining to the locations of the nearest restrooms or the restaurants with the cheapest prices needed to be answered. Some rangers liked that kind of duty, but it did not fulfill his dreams. Ethan wanted to be outdoors, exploring every nook and cranny of Yellowstone National Park – climbing its majestic mountain ranges and seeing the world-famous geysers and hot springs. He wanted to be as close as possible to the wildlife: grizzlies, black bears, foxes, moose, elk, buffalo, and wolves. He set his sights on being the first man to record the unexplored regions of the park, places in which no other human had yet to set foot. He did not want to be cooped up inside some tiny gatehouse, breathing in exhaust fumes. This was his dream job, after all ... ever since he was ten years old and his father had taken his younger brother, Mark, and him camping for the first time. He could still smell the woodsmoke from his first campfire and taste the hotdogs and crispy marshmallows. He remembered the ghost stories his father recounted in their tent late at night while he and his brother huddled close together in their sleeping bags.

Last night had been a ghost story of a different sort, though. The dream was still fresh in his mind. *Why wouldn't it be?* After all, he'd had the same nightmare for eleven straight days. *Rats. Rats were everywhere. Shiny black bodies with pink tails, twisting and swarming in giant masses. Their tiny-black, lifeless eyes looking at me. Mouths opening and closing, showing razor sharp teeth. They seemed to be waiting for something. A signal. What was it they were waiting for? Why did they never attack me?* Each night he woke from the nightmare, drenched in sweat, before the answer could reveal itself. Somehow, he knew deep in his soul that whatever they were waiting for, whatever signal, would one day make itself known.

Outside of his window, the cries from hungry mouths rescued him from reliving more of the dream. In the large pine tree near his cabin, red-headed woodpeckers were roosting, and their brood were crying for their breakfast. Ethan went to the stove and filled his coffee mug to the brim. No sugar or cream for him. He liked it black and strong, identical to the way his father used to make it.

Walking outside, he took in the view. The rangers' living arrangements were situated near a ridgeline of enormous pine trees. Above the ridgeline were barren hills hiding a box canyon he wished to explore at his first opportunity. The wind was still blowing cold and strong, but the clouds were moving off. It appeared his luck was holding as far as the weather was concerned. He took a sip of his coffee and glanced down the dirt path lined with painted white rocks flanking neat rows of small brush that led from his cabin to the ranger headquarters, some two hundred yards away. Housed inside the ranger headquarters were the offices of the Chief of Rangers, Dustin Miller, and Captain Steven J. Herrmann, along with the communications center run by Lieutenant Fred Spanyer, a hard-ass if ever there was one. At various intervals stood a chow hall and several more log cabins used as bunkhouses for more rangers. A tendril of smoke coming from the chimney of the chow hall announced the cook was awake and preparing breakfast. One of the many perks of being a ranger was the first-rate food, at least in his opinion. The smell of bacon cooking lured Ethan down the trail to the chow hall, but a fresh pile of bear scat caused him to stop in his tracks. Suddenly wary of his surroundings, he scanned the pine trees. Nothing. The scat, from his estimation, was no more than an hour old, perhaps even less. He had left his sidearm locked in his footlocker back at the cabin. *Rookie mistake.* Scat on the trail was nothing new to him, of course. As a rookie ranger, it was one of his jobs to keep the trail clean of droppings. He had seen moose and deer droppings on the trail, even fox, but never bear. This appeared to be a huge one. Maybe even a grizzly. His eyes darted to where the dumpster was fenced in. The gate was still closed, and the padlock appeared to be in place. He had heard the stories of large bears breaking the locks on fences and overturning heavy dumpsters in their constant quest for food.

'You see something interesting in that there dumpster, boy?'

Startled, Ethan looked to where the voice had come from. It was the cook, Jambe, standing outside the front door of the chow hall, wearing his usual a cowboy hat and moccasins get-up. 'Morning, Jambe. I saw some bear scat on the path. Looked to be a large one, and I thought he might still be in the area.'

'You rookies are all alike. Scared of your own shadow. That's grizzly poop, boy. I watched him take a shit from where I'm standing. He's long gone now.'

'You saw him?' Ethan asked flatly.

'Didn't I just say so? He was snooping around here when I opened the mess hall less than an hour ago. Big one, too. Looked to be about eight feet tall, and a good seven hundred pounds, give or take. He took off for parts unknown when he heard my shotgun lock in a round, though. Smart bear. Otherwise, you rangers would be having some fresh bear stew for lunch tomorrow.'

Ethan glared at the cook. 'You'd have shot him?'

'No shit. I'd have shot him real good. Bear that big got no business being around here, and I don't care to have him sneaking up on me when I'm not paying attention. Come inside, and I'll make you up something special on the stove.'

Ethan frowned. The thought of Jambe shooting the grizzly for any reason other than self-defense disturbed him deeply, but he obliged the cook and went inside the mess hall.

The dining area was laid out in a large rectangle with roughhewn tables lining the walls. There was enough seating for seventy-five men. A massive stone fireplace decorated with several sets of huge elk and deer antlers was the central focus of the room. A roaring fire gave the mess hall a warm and cozy feeling and helped to starve off the morning chill.

'So, what would you like this morning, Ethan? Steak? Maybe some thick ham? Or how about some bacon?'

'Steak, medium-well, sounds good, Jambe.'

'How about your eggs? How many, and what style suits you?'

'Three, over-easy, please.'

'Toast?' asked Jambe.

'Sure. Thank you.'

'No problem. That's why I'm here, Ethan. Pour us both some coffee, and let's have a talk, you and me.'

'Sure thing. Anything in particular you have in mind you'd like to discuss?'

'There is something on my mind, Ethan. I heard talk around camp that you've got yourself a new assignment taking some of them scientist fellas around the park for a few weeks. Any truth in that rumor?'

'Yeah, Jambe. That's true. So, what?'

'Don't you sass-talk me, boy. You just answer my questions before I box your ears, understand?'

'Yes, sir.'

'That's better. Do you have any idea what they might be poking around for?'

'No, sir. All the chief told me was that I was to escort them anywhere they wanted to visit and to keep a logbook of their activities.'

'Their activities, huh?' grunted Jambe with a look of disapproval on his weathered face.

'Yes. Anything wrong, Jambe?'

I surely don't know, but I don't like it one bit. About seven or eight years back, long before your time, some of them scientists came poking around here.'

'Poking? What do you mean by *poking* around here?' asked Ethan.

'If'n you'd shut your mouth for a spell, I'd tell you.'

'Sorry, Jambe. I'm listening.'

'Them scientists were poking around the park looking for any sign that Yellowstone might be close to erupting.'

Ethan interrupted, 'You need a volcano for an eruption, Jambe. I think someone was pulling your leg seven years ago.'

Jambe snapped, 'You sure is ignorant, boy. Where did you go to school? Don't you know you're having breakfast right now on top of the world's largest, active super volcano?'

Ethan chuckled, 'Now, you're pulling my leg, Jambe.'

'Look it up, dumb shit. You have a computer in your cabin, don't you?'

Ethan scoffed, 'Say you're right about all this, and I'm not saying you are. What's so wrong with them looking around the park?'

'Last time, them scientists closed down the park for near a whole month. Said they wanted to be on the safe side because of some disturbance their monitors had picked up. They even lied to the public, so as not to scare the hell out of everyone. Said the park was being closed for maintenance reasons.'

'So, what kind of *disturbance* were they talking about?' challenged Ethan.

'How the hell do I know what kind of disturbance? You think they came in here to my mess hall and discussed it over coffee with me? All I do know is that I went a full month without pay and had to sleep at my sister's house with her bratty kids making an endless racket.'

'Well, thanks for breakfast and the story, Jambe, but it's time for me to report to headquarters. The chief wants me in front of his desk at 0800 prompt.'

'So, get going then. What's stopping you? You just mind what you say to them there scientists. And report back to me what they're saying about this park ... if you ever want to have steak for breakfast again.'

* * *

Returning to his cabin to change into his uniform, Ethan reflected for a moment on what he had just learned. *A super volcano below his feet. Was that possible?* Of course, it was possible, but was it probable? One of his bunkmates, Joseph Anderson, stirred and sat up in bed, wiping the sleep from his eyes.

'Hey, Ethan. You're up early. Where've you been?'

'Went to the chow hall for an early breakfast. Hey, Joe, can I ask you a stupid question?'

'Sure, what's up?'

'When I was having breakfast, Jambe told me some wild tale about Yellowstone sitting on top of some super volcano. Do you know anything about that?'

'Sure, Ethan. Hell, I thought every ranger knew that was true. By the way, doesn't your new assignment start today?'

'Yeah. I'm about to head out. Have to be front and center in front of the chief at 0800.'

'You'd better get a move on. It's 0750, and you don't want to keep the old man waiting, or there will be hell to pay.'

'Thanks, Joe.
Later, Ranger.'

* * *

Upon his arrival at ranger headquarters, Ethan knocked on the office door of Dustin Miller, Chief of Rangers. For a brief moment, he felt apprehensive about the meeting, but it passed quickly. The door was opened by Captain Herrmann.

'Come in and take a seat.'

'Thank you, sir.'

Seated around a large conference table were Chief of Rangers Miller, Lt. Fred Spanyer, two older gentlemen, and a young woman. Ethan surmised the people he did not know as the scientists he was to escort around Yellowstone.

'Glad to see that you're punctual, Ranger Hardy', said the chief.

Ethan took his seat. 'I always try to be, sir.'

Chief Miller continued, 'Before we start, let me introduce you to Dr. Ben Williams, Dr. Mark Stoner, and Dr. Stacey Peterson.'

Ethan studied the three for a moment. Dr. Williams was a tall, studious man whom Ethan guessed to be near sixty years old and very fit for his age. Dr. Stoner was a squat, bald man with round eyeglasses. He looked quite out of place in the wildness of the park. Hardy thought Stoner might be closer to seventy years old. Dr. Peterson looked nothing like a doctor with her long blond hair in a ponytail, blue eyes, and a swimsuit model's body. *This assignment's looking better and better*, Hardy thought to himself. Dr. Stoner stood and held out his boney hand.

'Ranger Hardy, we are all very happy to make your acquaintance. I hope you don't mind being taken away from your normal duties to babysit some scientists for a few weeks?'

Rising from his seat, Ethan shook Dr. Stoner's hand while stealing another quick glance at Dr. Peterson. 'Not at all, sir. I'm looking forward to the assignment. It will be a welcomed change of pace.'

Chief Miller shot Hardy a look of disapproval. 'If everyone would please take their seats, we will proceed with this meeting. Captain Herrmann, the floor is yours.'

'Thank you, Chief Miller.' Captain Herrmann stood and walked over to where a complete map of Yellowstone National Park hung on the wall. 'Ranger Hardy, your assignment is a simple one but important, nonetheless. For the next several weeks, you will serve as an escort for our guests. You will accompany them wherever they choose to visit within the boundaries of the areas circled in red on this map, which you will be supplied a copy of before you leave.'

'Excuse me, Captain Herrmann, but it was our understanding that there would be no restrictions on where we choose to go,' challenged Dr. Williams.

Herrmann studied Dr. Williams for a moment. 'The reason for the restrictions, Dr. Williams, is for your group's safety. We have had two bear attacks in recent weeks. One of them was fatal and quite vicious, I might add. We can't have you and your party going into those areas at this time. I am very sorry if this causes you any inconvenience.'

'While we appreciate your concern for our safety, Captain, I must insist that there be no restrictions of any sort on where we decide to travel,' countered Dr. Williams.

Chief Miller grunted. 'I have to agree with Captain Herrmann. Travel into known bear territory, especially after these recent attacks, would be a very bad idea, Dr. Williams. We must err on the side of caution at this time.'

Dr. Ben Williams turned in his chair to face the chief. 'Chief Miller, I have the utmost respect for both you and your staff's opinion, but you have your orders from Washington. We are to be given your complete cooperation, along with total access to all regions of the park. If it is a question of safety, then might I suggest another ranger or two accompany us?'

Chief Miller cleared his throat and stared hard at Dr. Williams. 'Of course, sir. As you have stated, I have my orders. Lt. Spanyer, you will also serve as escort for the party.'

Spanyer scowled, 'Sir, with all due respect, what about my duties as communications officer?'

'Communications can be covered by Captain Herrmann in your absence. Are there any other questions, Lieutenant?' demanded the chief.

'No, sir. None at this time.'

Chief Miller gave a grim nod. 'Good. Let's conclude this meeting. Ranger Hardy, Lt. Spanyer will now be accompanying you, and he will fill you in on the details of your assignment. There are two fully-outfitted camper trucks parked outside. Lt. Spanyer, you will drive one; Hardy, you will drive the other. Both trucks contain enough food and water to last a minimum of two weeks. When supplies run low, radio in your location, and I will see to it that you are resupplied. Both of you will carry your normal sidearm. In addition, a shotgun and satellite radio are equipped in each camper. Lt. Spanyer, you have ten minutes to pack.'

* * *

Ethan climbed in behind the wheel of the Ford he was assigned. Dr. Williams took the passenger seat next to him, and Dr. Peterson sat in the rear. Lt. Spanyer and Dr. Stoner were already under way in the lead.

Stacey shifted uneasily in her seat. 'The meeting could have been handled more professionally, Ben.'

There was a smug look of satisfaction on his face. 'Meaning what, Stacey?'

'Telling Chief Miller that he had his orders from Washington sounded almost like a threat. You should have been more diplomatic.'

'I am a scientist, Stacey, not a diplomat. If you don't like the way I handle things, too bad. I happen to be in charge of this little excursion. Please don't make the mistake of thinking otherwise.'

'I beg your pardon?' she fired back.

'Meaning ... if you don't want to spend the rest of your days stuck inside an eight-by-ten office with no windows to the outside world and no prospect of ever doing field work again while you're employed by U.S.G.S., please keep your opinions to yourself unless you are asked, which I don't plan on doing much of.'

An uncomfortable silence followed as Ethan put the truck in gear and followed Spanyer out of the ranger compound and onto the paved roadway. The sky had turned a brilliant shade of blue as the last of the clouds moved off, leaving behind the promise of a beautiful day. Ethan decided to see if he could thaw the temperature inside the truck. 'What exactly will you be doing out in the field, Dr. Williams, if you don't mind my asking, sir?'

'Well, Ranger Hardy, we are scientists, as you must be aware of by now. Volcanologists, to be exact. We work for the U.S.G.S. and need to check and update our seismographs located throughout Yellowstone. Perhaps even making some minor repairs, if need be. And no, I don't mind questions, so long as they are intelligent ones.'

'Well, sir, my first question would be what does U.S.G.S. stand for?'

'That would be your second question, Ranger Hardy,' countered Dr. Williams.

'My second question, sir?'

'You first asked what we would be doing out in the field, and I have already provided you with the answer to that question.'

'Yes, sir. I see what you mean,' Ethan murmured.

'To answer your second question, U.S.G.S. stands for United States Geological Survey. Dr. Peterson and I are assigned to the Denver Federal Office, while Dr. Stoner is assigned to the main office in Reston, Virginia.'

A huge moose and her baby calf casually walked across the roadway in front of the campers. Both vehicles slowed and came to a complete stop as the moose appeared to be in no hurry.

Stacey came alive at the sight of the moose and her calf. 'Oh my! Can I get out to take a picture, please?'

Ethan obliged by pulling the truck off the road. 'Don't get to close, Dr. Peterson,' Ethan advised.

'It's Stacey.'

He gave her a surprised look.

'Please call me by my first name, and if you don't mind, I'll call you by yours instead of Ranger-this or Ranger-that.'

'Sure, Stacey. It suits me just fine. You had better hurry with that picture. Moose aren't known for being the most social of animals.'

'Oh. Yes, of course. Thank you, Ethan.' Stacey Peterson stepped down from the truck and went as close to the moose as she dared.

Both mother and baby stared her way with suspicious eyes but soon began grazing by the side of the roadway with only an occasional glance in her direction.

Dr. Williams sighed dramatically. 'Ranger Hardy, may I ask you a direct question?'

'What's on your mind, sir?'

'You find Dr. Peterson to be very attractive, don't you?'

Hardy shifted uneasily in his seat. 'Sir?'

'Come now, Ranger Hardy. We're both men of the world. I noticed the way you were looking at her at ranger headquarters, and the way you're watching her now. My advice to you would be to simply forget any romantic ideas you might have forming inside your head. She's way out of your league, young man. Besides, my guess is you're around twenty-two or twenty-three years old. Stacey is thirty-two, and I know for a fact that she prefers older, more mature men.'

Ethan stared hard at Dr. Williams. 'I have to speak bluntly, sir. What business would it be of yours if I *were* interested in Stacey?'

'Well, young man, to get right to the point of the matter, Stacey and I are involved with each other and have been for over two years. Does that answer your impertinent question?'

Ethan was dumbstruck. 'I'm very sorry, sir. I had no idea that the two of you were involved with each other.'

'Your apology is accepted, Ranger Hardy. Let's have no more discussion about the matter.'

'Of course not, sir.'

Stacey climbed back into her seat, flush with excitement. 'Wow! Did you see how close I was to them? I got some great pictures. Thank you so much for stopping, Ethan.'

'You're welcome, Stacey. Anytime.'

'What did you two boys talk about while I was out of the truck?'

Williams chuckled softly. 'Nothing much, Stacey. Ranger Hardy was just inquiring about the location of our first stop, and I was about to inform him of it when you got back into the camper. Ranger Hardy, our first stop will be ...'

Stacey interrupted, 'Oh, Ben, can you please stop referring to Ethan as Ranger Hardy? It sounds too formal. After all, we're going to be working together for several weeks.'

Williams gave Stacey a look of irritation. 'I have told you more times than I care to remember that I don't like to be interrupted, Stacey. Once again, please try to remember that.'

'I'm very sorry, Ben,' Stacey murmured.

'Well, Ranger Hardy, is it agreeable with you if I call you by your first name?'

Hardy gave a casual shrug. 'That would be fine with me, sir.'

Williams paused for a moment before continuing, 'If there are no more interruptions, I'll answer your question about our destinations. Our first stop will be Norris Geyser Basin. Are you familiar with that region, Ethan?'

'I know about the area, sir, but I've never been there before. I have put in a lot of study time concerning various regions of Yellowstone, though.'

Williams gave a wan nod of approval. 'Let us test your knowledge, then. What can you tell us about Norris Geyser Basin?'

'Well, sir, as I'm sure you're aware, it's the oldest and hottest active region of the park.'

'Very good, Ethan. Our second stop will be the Upper Geyser Basin. What can you tell us about this area?' continued Dr. Williams.

'That's an easy one, sir. That's where Old Faithful is located, along with well-over one hundred other geysers.'

'Right again, although the number of geysers is closer to 180. Now for the hard one, Ethan. Mary Bay. What do you know about Mary Bay?'

'I've never heard of Mary Bay, sir.'

'That's understandable, young man. Few people have. Mary Bay is the hottest spot in Yellowstone Lake with a recorded temperature of 252 °F.'

'Besides those three areas, will we be going anywhere else, Dr. Williams?' inquired Ethan.

'Those three are the main regions we want to hit. In addition, we need to stop at Midway, West Thumb, Shoshone, and Heart Lake Geyser basins. If you don't mind, Ethan, I would like to close my eyes and rest until we reach our first destination.'

SEVEN

BRUCK AN DER MUR, AUSTRIA.

June 6, 2030.

Edmund Kretz swung his heavy axe and split the log cleanly in two. Arching to stretch his back, he grabbed the dirty rag from his back pocket and wiped the sweat from his forehead and chest. It was still mid-morning, but the sun was already high overhead and burning hot upon him. He cursed under his breath. *When would things get better for his small family? Every day was a struggle to put meat on the table for his wife and three small children.* He was a carpenter by trade, like his father and grandfather. He had learned his profession working side-by-side with both of them. His passion, though, was crafting fine furniture; however, any work would do: mending broken fences, putting shingles on roofs, or splitting logs as he was doing now. Like his father and grandfather, Edmund was a poor man. Today's work would only bring in enough money for a small bottle of milk for baby Ada, a loaf of bread, and perhaps some sweet butter for the twins to have for lunch. He needed to hunt or fish for his family's dinner tonight. Hunting ... it provided him with the excuse to search for hidden treasure. First things first, though. He neatly stacked the logs he had split near his neighbor's barn as he had been instructed to do.

'So, you have finally finished your work with those logs, have you?'

Edmund glanced up. 'Yes, Frederica. They are stacked by your barndoor, nice and neat, just the way you like them to be.'

'Put your shirt back on. You know my husband doesn't like you walking around his farm, half-dressed like that,' Frederica replied, blushing.

Edmund laughed. 'But what about you, sweet one? Do you like me this way?'

'I am an old woman of seventy-four, and you are a strong young man no older than a son to me. Behave yourself before I tell your wife about the way you act.'

'Ah, lovely Frederica. My wife, Sophia, knows how much I adore you. You would not be telling her anything that she is not already well aware of.'

'Hush, Edmund. I have your pay, here in my pocket, and some bread and jam with goat's milk to wash it down with. How is Sophia, by the way? I have not seen her for a few days.'

'She is well. Baby Ada keeps her busy, and Johannes and Christian are a handful to deal with, as nine-year-old boys sometimes are.'

'If you look over your shoulder, you might see the twins coming across the pasture with my dear husband in tow. Where could they have been off to, I wonder?'

'Causing mischief, no doubt,' Edmund replied with a tight smile. He waved to his sons. 'Come on, boys. Show me which one of you is faster.'

The twins, hearing their father's challenge, took off running across the meadow. Christian, out of breath and gasping for air, was the first to jump into his father's strong arms. 'Papa, you will never guess where we've been this morning and what we have found!'

'Let me tell him! Let me tell him! I was the one who found the cave,' proclaimed Johannes breathlessly as he arrived right behind his brother.

'Whoa, little man. Catch your breath. What is all this talk of a cave? Where have my two sons been off exploring this morning?'

Josef Kronenberg, his aged face flushed with excitement and exhaustion from the long walk, caught up with the twins. 'It is true, Edmund. I saw the entrance to the cave, myself.'

Both twins spun around, but Johannes was the first to speak. 'Uncle Josef, let me tell Papa.'

'As you wish, Johannes, but be quick about it before you and your brother burst with the news,' chuckled Josef.

'Papa, we found a cave close by the train tracks. It was dark inside. I wanted to go in, but Uncle Josef said no. He said there might be snakes or bats inside. I wasn't afraid, but I think Christian was a little bit.'

'I wasn't afraid. Uncle said we weren't allowed to go in,' countered Christian.

'You two boys have had enough excitement for one morning,' scolded Frederica. 'Into the house, both of you, and wash your hands with soap and hot water. I'll have some faschingskrapfen and milk waiting for you both after you have finished cleaning up.'

Josef sat down on his work bench with a heavy sigh and took out his pipe and tobacco.

'So, Josef, tell me all about this *cave* my sons have discovered,' Edmund asked with a touch of exuberance in his voice.

Josef lit his pipe and drew the smoke in deeply before exhaling it out slowly. 'I was standing outside the Kornmesser House three nights past, and I overheard a rumor.' He paused for effect. 'Seems that Bohn found a small, one-ounce gold bar with the swastika stamped on it sometime late last week while he was out walking the old rail line with that metal detector of his.'

'I heard the same rumor, and that's all it is. Old-man Bohn has spent his whole life searching for Nazi treasure and not a coin to show for it. Besides, no one has seen the gold bar, have they?'

'No. No one has. That much is true, my friend, and no one has seen Bohn since he spoke about it either.'

'Meaning what?' challenged Edmund.

'Meaning, I think he went back out into the woods by those train tracks looking around some more. Maybe even near that cave the twins and I found. You and I have done our own searching for many years, also. Neither of us have ever seen this cave. It is a known fact that those Nazi bastards used that rail line, and it's also a known fact they buried stolen artwork, gold, and silver in this area.'

'We know they used the rail line. For what purpose, no one knows. As far as it supposedly being a known fact there's any treasure buried around here, well, that's only wishful thinking on both of our parts, Josef.'

Josef puffed on his pipe and let the smoke out in a tight circle. 'Do you want to go search the cave with me or not, Edmund? If you say no, I'll go inside alone; although, I am hoping you will go with me.'

Edmund cleared his throat and spat in the dust. 'You know I will go with you, old man. It's just ... well, let's not get our hopes up too high. As you said, we have both looked for many years and don't have a single coin to show for our effort.'

They walked without another word into the large farmhouse. Frederica and the twins were sitting at the kitchen table enjoying their treat.

'I guess you two will be outdoors the rest of the day.' She gave them a knowing smile.

Josef bent over and gave his wife a tender kiss on the forehead. 'We will be back in time for supper, my dear. Have Sophia bring the baby over and join us for the evening meal and prayer.'

* * *

The cave's entrance was less than a half a mile from the abandoned railroad tracks. Looking at the opening, Edmund could see why he and Josef had missed it and wondered how the twins had discovered it. Weeds and brush choked the dark maw, and at some point, in the distant past, a huge fir tree had fallen, blocking it even more. Turning on his flashlight, Josef peered inside. His light, as powerful as it was, did little to penetrate the inky darkness.

'Shine your light in here, too, Edmund.'

With both lights now probing the cave, the two men could just make out the dimensions and depth before them. The cave sloped downward, and there was more than enough room for them to stand up at full height with no danger of bumping their heads on the cavern's ceiling. A damp, unpleasant smell greeted their arrival.

'Someone has been in here recently,' declared Josef, pointing at footprints clearly visible in the mud.

'You think it might be Bohn?' asked Edmund.

'Who else could it be? From his tracks, it looks like he has gone back and forth quite a few times. I wonder if he is still in here?'

'There is only one way to find out, and he's not going to be happy to see either one of us,' muttered Edmund.

'That's too bad. He has no claim on anything we might find in here.'

'What I'd like to know is how he found this cave.' Edmund gave a grunt of annoyance. 'He may have seen you and the twins poking around here and decided to have a look inside for himself.'

Josef looked skeptically at his friend. 'The boys and I were here less than two hours ago. Judging from the amount of tracks I see, Bohn has been in here more than a few times. Maybe this is where he found that gold bar.'

Leaving the mouth of the cave, they walked carefully down the slope of the tunnel. They paused to listen from time-to-time, but the only sound they heard was the slow drip of water somewhere far beneath them. The floor of the cavern was damp and slippery, making every step treacherous. Edmund tilted his head back and played his flashlight across the rock overhead. To his inexperienced eye, the ceiling looked solid enough, but he was cautious, nonetheless.

Josef, who had the good sense to count his steps, paused for a moment to rest and catch his breath. 'I figure we have walked at least 300 yards by now,' he said, gasping for air.

Edmund glanced at his friend. 'Are you all right, old man? Your breathing is very heavy.'

'I'll be fine soon enough. Just let me stop for a minute. It's hot as hell in here and hard to breathe.'

Edmund leaned against the rock wall and rolled himself a smoke. For a moment, he thought he heard metal grinding on metal, but the sound ceased almost at once.

Josef gave him a surprised look. 'I heard it, too. I guess we are not alone down here after all.'

'Let's get moving and find out what made that noise,' grunted Edmund as he stepped on his cigarette.

They walked on another 60 paces when they came to a slight bend in the tunnel with a much steeper downward slope. They both paused to listen. The air was hot and thick. There was no sound except for the dripping water until they heard the unmistakable sound: a shovel hitting metal.

'Turn off your flashlight for a moment, Josef.'

In the pitch blackness, they both saw a dim light less than a hundred yards away, below where they stood. Keeping their flashlights off, they felt their way along the damp walls of the cave. In the soft light cast by several lanterns, they spied the figure of a man bent over, struggling to move a heavy rock. It was old-man Bohn.

Bohn had stacked several small boxes and placed them near where he was digging. The boxes were clearly marked with the Nazi swastika. Two of the boxes had been opened, and the glint of gold reflected in the poor light. *Treasure. Nazi treasure.* Edmund shifted his weight, and in doing so, dislodged several small rocks that tumbled to the chamber floor below them.

Startled, Bohn spun around. 'Who's there?

Edmund and Josef stepped forward and started down the slope.

'Take it easy, Bohn. It's just Edmund and me.'

'What do you want? You have no business being here.'

'We have as much right to be here as you do, Bohn, and we're not going away, so get used to the idea right now,' snapped Edmund.

'It's mine, I tell you. I was the one who found it,' Bohn grumbled.

As he reached the chamber floor, Edmund stared gravely at the old man. 'There is more than enough for the three of us to share, Bohn, and you know you can't make us go away. Besides, a man your age will need help getting all this out of here. Did you really believe you could move this heavy gold and silver by yourself?'

Bohn's shoulders slumped. He studied the two men standing before him for a moment. 'You have made a good argument, Edmund. There is more than enough here for the three of us. Hell, we couldn't spend this much in ten lifetimes. And I do need your help. That much is true.'

'Now you're talking sense, Bohn. The three of us are partners as of this moment,' declared Josef.

'What have you dug up so far?' asked Edmund. His voice was filled with excitement.

Bohn smiled. 'These five boxes: four are filled with gold bars, and one has silver.'

'My God. We're rich,' whispered Edmund.

'Are there any more besides these five boxes?' asked Josef.

In answer, Bohn picked up one of his lanterns and shone the light around the large cavern. In the soft glow, the light revealed dozens of large crates and small boxes stacked haphazardly around the walls of the large chamber. 'In those large crates are paintings. The smaller boxes hold more gold and silver bars from what I've been able to tell. I'm guessing they didn't have time to bury it all. I have located nine more areas with my metal detector. I was digging up the first spot when you both showed up.'

Edmund and Josef stood still as if they were in shock, staring around the cave, unable to speak a word. At last, Josef spoke in a hoarse voice barely above a whisper, 'I cannot believe what I am seeing. It's a dream come true.'

Edmund walked over to where the large crates had been placed against the wall of the cavern. He took out his large hunting knife and pried the lid off one. Inside, as if placed there yesterday, was a gilded frame. Pulling it carefully out of the box, the painting took his breath away. On a small notecard attached to the frame were the words: *The Lovers, Vincent Van Gogh*. Edmund put the painting back inside its crate and opened another. On that notecard were the words: *Portrait of a Young Man, Raphael*.

Josef walked over, stood next to his friend, and put his hand on his shoulder. 'This is too much, Edmund. These paintings belong back in the museums from where they were stolen. We should tell the authorities what we have found.'

Edmund spun around to face his friend. 'What? They will take it all from us, and then where would I be? Back to cutting wood and worrying every night about how I will feed my boys and get milk for Ada. No. I won't hear of it. Do you understand me, Josef? I can feed my family now. I don't have to worry anymore.'

A slight scraping noise distracted Edmund. Turning, he saw a large rat perched on one of the containers. With a look of disgust, he bent over, picked up a heavy rock, and brought it down hard, breaking the rat's back.

'Why did you do that, Edmund?' asked Bohn. 'That was one of God's creatures. It is a grave sin to kill for no purpose.'

'I hate rats. They serve no purpose and are foul creatures. Enough talk. Let's start moving some of this gold out of the cave and get it home before nightfall,' Edmund demanded.

More scraping noises behind the men caused them all to turn. A half dozen rats were sitting atop the crates ... then a dozen ... and then twenty more. The three men looked all around them. Large black rats were everywhere. They poured out of every crevice and blocked the entrance to the cavern as if they somehow knew it was the only way out. There were hundreds; black eyes stared at the three men from every direction. As if on signal, the rats moved toward them in unison, stalking them like prey.

A larger one jumped from a nearby crate and sunk its teeth into Josef's neck. His scream of pain seemed to trigger something within the rats. They swarmed the three men; their sharp teeth ripped into flesh. The sound of screaming faded quickly, replaced by the sound of teeth gnawing on bone. No more problems ... no more worries ...

EIGHT

YELLOWSTONE NATIONAL PARK, WYOMING.

June 7, 2030.

Stacey pulled back the flap of her tent and peered outside. *Beautiful.* In every direction, Mother Nature had outdone herself. Their camp was on a high bluff overlooking the north shore of Shoshone Lake. Willows, flowers, and shrubs in multiple shades of green and yellow speckled the edges of the lake. A large bull moose was standing in the shallows, feeding on the foliage. It lifted its massive head, tested the scent in the air, and resumed eating. The tangy smell of woodsmoke caught her attention. Ethan, with his back to her, was bent over the firepit coaxing a small blaze to life. She watched him silently for a few moments. Not for the first time, she noticed his broad shoulders and all-American, boy-next-door good looks. She chastised herself. *He is way too young for you, Stacey Peterson.* Sensing someone's presence, Ethan turned around. Their eyes met, and Stacey felt herself blush. *He caught me looking at him like some freshman school girl.* Ethan gave her a shy smile.

'Good morning, Stacey. Would you care for a cup of coffee?'

'That would be nice, Ethan. Thank you,' she replied. Her cheeks still felt warm.

Ethan poured a steaming mug-full of coffee and handed it to her. 'Looks like it's going to be a picture-perfect day. Did you happen to notice the bull moose down by the shore?'

'Oh, yes! It's huge. I think I'll get my camera and take his picture.' Stacey put her cup down on a flat rock and went back to her tent.

Ethan glanced down by the shore. 'Never mind the camera, Stacey. He's already gone.'

'Well, if I can't take his picture, then how about yours?' Stacey laughed and snapped a few quick shots.

'That's not fair. I haven't had time to comb my hair this morning. What would you like me to make you for breakfast before everyone else rolls out of their sleeping bags?'

'Why don't you let me make the meal, Ethan? After all, you've been doing all the cooking since we have been in the field,' she replied with a mischievous glint in her eyes.

'I didn't know that scientists knew how to cook, but I'm willing to be your guinea pig.'

'Well, mister, have a seat, and I'll show you what a scientist can do. How do you like your eggs?'

'Not burned would be a nice start. But to answer your question, over easy. Thank you for doing this. It's very nice of you.'

'No problem. I'll try not to burn your eggs too badly, wise guy.'

Ethan watched her in silence as she busied herself with the eggs and bacon. He admired that she wasted no movements in her actions. Stacey glanced over at him, and they exchanged smiles. Handing over his plate, they took a seat near the fire, not too close, but not too far apart either.

'So, Ranger Hardy, does my cooking meet with your approval?'

'Well, yes and no. I like my bacon crispier. Overall, not a bad job.'

She gave him a playful punch in the arm. 'Asshole.'

Ethan let out a tragic sigh that was clearly feigned. 'Yes. Yes I am.'

Stacey swallowed nervously. 'Do you mind if I ask you a direct question?'

'Is that how every scientist starts a conversation when they want to ask a personal question?'

She shot him a quizzical look. 'What do you mean by that?'

Ethan hesitated before answering. 'Dr. Williams asked me a question in that same manner,' he blurted.

'Well, I was just going to ask you how old you are. I doubt very much if it was the same question Ben was going to ask. What *did* he want to know?'

Ethan looked surprised by the question. 'I'm 23 ... 24 in August. I'd rather not discuss the conversation I had with Dr. Williams. It makes me a little bit uncomfortable.'

'I'd really like to know what you and Ben were talking about.'

Ethan shifted uncomfortably in his seat. 'He asked me if I thought you were attractive.'

Stacey smiled. 'Do you?'

'Are you kidding? You're beautiful,' Ethan gushed too quickly.

'Thanks. That's very sweet of you. Is that what you told Ben? That you thought I was beautiful?'

'I don't think I answered the question, directly. I asked him what business it was of his.'

'Somehow, knowing Ben the way I do, I don't think your boldness went over too well with him.' Stacey refilled his plate with eggs, bacon, and hash browns. 'Did he say anything else?' she continued.

'He said the two of you are dating each other and have been for a couple of years.'

Stacey Peterson paused with a look of distress clouding her face. 'We *were* involved with each other for just over two years, but it ended a few weeks ago. This research trip had already been assigned by the main office in Virginia, and Dr. Stoner had requested us both personally ... I couldn't back out on this assignment, especially since it's significant for my career.'

'I'm sorry. I should have kept my mouth shut.'

'It's not your fault. After all, I pressed you about it, and I'm afraid Ben hasn't quite come to grips with our recent breakup.'

A rustling sound interrupted any further discussion. Lt. Spanyer, followed by the two doctors, emerged from their tents. 'The coffee smells good, Hardy,' grunted Lt. Spanyer. 'Did you save any for the rest of us to enjoy?'

'Yes, sir. There's plenty. Should I pour each of you a cup?'

Dr. Williams glanced from Evan to Stacey and back again. 'I can make my own coffee, Ethan, but thank you for asking. I see you're having breakfast, but Stacey is not. Why is that?'

'I made Ethan his breakfast, Ben. I thought it would be nice if someone cooked for him for a change,' Stacey murmured.

Dr. Williams scowled then he shrugged his shoulders with mock indifference. 'How cozy. Perhaps you wouldn't mind making all of us something to eat?'

'That's my job, sir. I'll make breakfast,' countered Ethan.

'Nonsense, Ethan. If Stacey can cook breakfast for you, then she should do it for everyone else,' challenged Dr. Williams.

'I don't mind, and I enjoy cooking,' Stacey pleaded.

Ethan swallowed hard, and without another word, nodded his consent.

After all the plates were collected, Dr. Williams and Dr. Stoner sat huddled near the small campfire, discussing their plans for the day while Stacey retreated into her tent to prepare her backpack.

'Leave the cleanup for a few minutes, Hardy, and take a walk with me. We need to talk,' said Lt. Spanyer.

'Yes, sir. Of course.'

As they walked through the dense fir and towering pine trees toward the lake below them, the only sound to be heard was made by their boots on the gravel. A stir of movement caused them both to stop and tilt their heads upward. Overhead, a bald eagle had taken flight, no doubt in search of prey.

Lt. Spanyer took his packet of chewing tobacco from his shirt pocket, pinched a wad between his index finger and thumb, and stuffed it into his mouth. He turned toward Ethan, his face contorted in a grimace. 'I'm not much good at talking one-on-one with people, Hardy, as I'm sure you're aware of by now. I'll keep this as brief as possible. I don't know what's going on with you, Dr. Williams, and the young lady. Truth be told, it's none of my business, and I make it a point not to interfere in other people's lives; however, I'd appreciate it if there were no problems while we're out in the field.'

'I'm sorry, sir. For my part, there won't be any trouble. I, of course, can't speak for Dr. Williams and his intentions.'

Lt. Spanyer cleared his throat and spat out some tobacco juice in the dirt. 'I understand you can't speak for another man, Hardy. Do me a favor and keep your distance from Williams as much as possible. Something's eating at that guy, and from what the chief told me, he's a powerful man with a lot of connections in Washington. We don't need the kind of problems he can cause us here at the park. Let's get back to the campsite and get this show on the road.'

Stacey was exiting her tent as they arrived back at camp. Ethan noticed that her blond hair was pulled back into a ponytail like the day they met. Her backpack was slung over her shoulder, and she seemed anxious to be underway. *Were her eyes red? Had she been crying?*

Stacey glanced at Ethan and Spanyer as they made their way back up the trail. 'Where have you two rangers been?' she asked coyly.

Ethan gave her a somber look. Taking a closer look, he was certain she had been crying. 'We just went for a short walk. It looks like you're ready to hit the trail.'

Stacey quickly put on a pair of sunglasses. 'Yep. I'm ready for anything Yellowstone has to offer.'

Lt. Spanyer walked over to the fire and doused it. 'Dr. Williams, what's the plan of action for today?'

Williams gazed up at Spanyer without an immediate response. He seemed annoyed by the lieutenant's presence. 'Dr. Stoner and I would like to visit the Shoshone Geyser Basin area along with Union, Minute Man, and Taurus geysers. We must check the seismographs in those areas and take some rock samples. If, of course, that meets with your approval.'

'You and Dr. Stoner are in charge, as you have made quite clear on a number of occasions. We will need to take two canoes to reach Shoshone Basin. It's too long of a hike from where we are now.'

'Please see to our transportation, Lieutenant. We will be ready to leave as soon as you give us the word,' replied Williams.

Spanyer felt his temper rising but held it in check. 'As you wish, Dr. Williams.' Turning, Spanyer motioned to Ethan, 'Get your backpack and sidearm on ... and help me get the canoes into the water.'

Williams poked the ashes in the firepit for a moment and chuckled under his breath.

Dr. Stoner shot Williams an angry look. 'Ben, you and I have been close friends and colleagues for nearly twenty-one years. I love you like a brother, but sometimes, you can be such a jackass.'

Williams sighed dramatically. 'I know, Mark. But I enjoy it tremendously, and I have to keep these two Neanderthals in their place. I doubt either of them have more than a high school education or an IQ above 110. Regardless, if it will make you feel better, I'll try my best not to be as big of a jackass for the remainder of our time in the field.'

With a high-pitched screech, the bald eagle returned to its nest with a rabbit clutched tightly in its talons. Beneath Union Geyser, deep underground, the earth shifted slightly.

* * *

Shoshone Lake was as smooth as glass, except for a few ripples lapping the shoreline. Ethan slid the two canoes into the water and tethered them to a large oak stump. Lt. Spanyer, who had started to load both canoes with knapsacks and canteens, paused for a moment to stretch his back and put a fresh wad of chew into his mouth. Spanyer glanced at his watch without paying it any sort of attention.

'That Williams is a real son-of-a-bitch, isn't he, Hardy?'

Ethan cleared his throat, 'I'm not sure how to respond to that question, sir. After all, he's an important scientist, and I'm just a rookie park ranger.'

Spanyer heaved a heavy sigh of exasperation. 'It's just the two of us standing near a lake, Hardy. You can speak your mind freely.'

'Well, in that case ... yes, sir. He's a real son-of-a-bitch, all right.'

Spanyer laughed and slapped Ethan on the back. 'That wasn't so hard now, was it? Listen to me. I want you and Dr. Stoner in one canoe, and I'll take the good Dr. Williams and Dr. Peterson in mine.' Spanyer squinted back up the trail toward their campsite. 'They are on their way down. Let's make it a good outing, Ranger Hardy. Try to enjoy the day.'

As Stacey approached the canoes, she gave Ethan a quick smile. She was still wearing her sunglasses, but Ethan noticed a slight puffing under her eyes.

Lt. Spanyer motioned toward his canoe. 'Dr. Williams, you and Dr. Peterson will ride with me. Dr. Stoner will ride with Ranger Hardy.'

Williams nodded. 'Are we prepared to leave, Lieutenant?'

'One thing, sir. Ranger Hardy and I will handle the paddles, of course. We ask that the three of you stay in the middle of the canoe at all times and refrain from making any sudden movements. Some parts of Shoshone Lake are well over 200 feet deep.'

Williams gave a grumble of annoyance. 'We have all been in canoes before on *many* occasions, Lieutenant, but thank you for your words of caution. Besides, we will all be wearing life vests.'

Ben Williams took Stacey's hand and helped her step into the canoe. Then he joined her, followed by Lt. Spanyer.

Ethan assisted Dr. Stoner, who appeared uncertain about how to enter the canoe. Once the canoes were untied from the tree stump, both he and Spanyer pushed off with strong strokes.

Williams turned around to face Spanyer. 'How long will it take us to reach our destination, Lieutenant?'

'We should reach shore in about fifteen to twenty minutes, depending on the current, sir. Off-road vehicles have been stored for our use at a nearby ranger station, so we can drive you to Shoshone and Union geysers, as well as anywhere else you would like to visit today.'

Dr. Williams grunted his approval and fell into a moody silence. Stacey, for her part, seemed to be enjoying every moment out on the lake, even going so far as to ask Lt. Spanyer if she could take a turn with the paddle. Spanyer obliged with a few words of instruction and caution. In a smooth rhythm, she propelled the canoe forward at a steady pace – showing everyone she was no novice. As they came around a small bend, a large bull elk feeding in the shallows lifted his head to stare at the intruders. Water dripped from its muzzle as it let out a loud bugle call of warning. Stacey relinquished the paddle back to Spanyer, and with a child's delight, began snapping pictures. The elk stamped its hoof as if in protest and disappeared into the nearby tree line.

'Stacey, do you plan on taking photographs of every creature we encounter?' Williams asked with a smirk.

Stacey nodded enthusiastically. 'Absolutely. They're so magnificent. Don't you think, Ben?'

Williams gazed at her and gave his standard dramatic sigh. 'I think that it's an embarrassing waste of time. How much longer before we reach your ranger station, Lt. Spanyer?'

'It's right around the next bend, Dr. Williams ... a few more minutes.'

As they rounded the bend in the river, the ranger's cabin came into view with its short wooden pier that extended fifteen feet out over the lake. On the pier, two young rangers were sitting on lounge chairs, each with a fishing pole in one hand and a can of beer in the other. They both stood at once as Lt. Spanyer's canoe came into view.

'At ease, rangers. I don't mind that you're fishing. I used to do some fishing myself from this very same pier when I was stationed here years ago. However, I do insist you drink on your own time. Tie our canoes to the pier and help our guests disembark,' snapped Spanyer.

As the two rangers secured the canoes to a wooden post, Ethan assisted Dr. Stoner onto the dock.

Stoner glanced shyly at Ethan. 'Thank you, young man. You've been most kind.'

'You're more than welcome, sir. Anything I can do to help, just let me know.'

Stoner motioned Ethan off to one side. 'Your lieutenant seems to have quite the reputation with the young rangers, Ethan. Even I find him to be somewhat intimidating.'

'Well, sir, I used to think he was intimidating until spending some time with him on this trip. I think his bark is much worse than his bite.'

'I wonder if you would do me a small favor, Ethan.'

'Of course, Dr. Stoner.'

'Would you please ask the lieutenant to hang back from the group for a minute, so I might have a word with him in private?'

'Is there anything wrong, sir?'

'Well, yes ... I mean, no. It is no complaint with you. I just wish to discuss a private matter with the lieutenant.'

As the small group made its way toward the cabin to freshen up and have lunch, Dr. Stoner remained on the dock. 'Are you coming, Mark?' asked Williams.

'I'll be along in a few minutes, Ben. I need a moment to collect myself. Save me some coffee, please.'

As they reached the cabin, Ethan touched Spanyer lightly on his shoulder. 'Excuse me, sir, but Dr. Stoner wants to have a word with you.'

Spanyer looked over his shoulder toward the pier. 'What's this all about, Hardy?'

'I don't know, sir. He wouldn't discuss it with me.'

Spanyer spun on his heel and headed back down the short path, muttering under his breath. As he reached the pier, Spanyer stared hard at Dr. Stoner. 'You wanted to have a word with me, sir. Is there a problem?'

'I'm very sorry to be so mysterious, Lieutenant. There is no problem with you or young Ethan, I assure you. I wanted to apologize on behalf of Dr. Williams for his rudeness. I've known Ben for over twenty years, Lieutenant. He's a fine man and a brilliant scientist, but he can also be more than a little arrogant. It's also my understanding that he and Dr. Peterson were involved with each other, and that they are going through a difficult time right now.'

Spanyer scowled for a moment but replaced it with a thin smile. 'I appreciate what you've told me, sir. It helps me understand him a little better, and I will try to be more patient with him.'

After lunch, all five of them mounted their off-road vehicles. Lt. Spanyer drove lead again with Dr. Williams seated next to him and Stacey in the rear with her camera at the ready. Ethan and Dr. Stoner followed behind. The vehicles were open: no doors or roof; the sounds of the engines prevented any conversation until they reached their destination at Union Geyser. The forest around them was tight with pine trees and thick brush, but as they drew closer to the geyser, the ground opened up into bare patches, bleached ghostly white – free of any vegetation, which was in stark contrast to the lush green of the forest nearer the ranger station and Shoshone Lake. Dr. Williams was the first out of the truck. In his hand was a GPS device that gave him the exact location of the seismograph.

Dr. Stoner joined him with a puzzled expression on his face. 'Union Geyser has been dormant since the 1970s, Ben. There should be more growth around those three vents. Look at the pine trees around here. They appear almost dead.'

'I have eyes, Mark. Make yourself useful and help me find the damn seismograph. This piece of crap GPS doesn't appear to be working.'

Stacey got out of the truck and looked at Ethan with a worried expression on her face. 'Something's not right, Ethan. Did you notice there were no signs of wildlife? I didn't get a single picture on the way here.'

Ethan looked around. 'Well, the trucks are pretty loud. I'm sure we made enough noise to scare away every living creature for miles.'

Stacey seemed unconvinced. 'There aren't even any birds in the trees or sky as far as I can see. It's creepy. Everything is white and dead.'

Spanyer walked over to join them. 'What are you two talking about?'

'Sir, Stacey is worried about the appearance of the trees and the fact that there is no visible wildlife anywhere to be seen.'

Spanyer arched his eyebrows. 'The trees do look rather sickly. As for the animals, that's easy to explain. Those two trucks made enough noise to wake the dead. We scared the hell out of every deer or bear for a mile or more.'

Stacey glanced from Ethan to Spanyer. 'That doesn't explain why there are no birds, squirrels, or chipmunks. Can either one of you explain that?'

Dr. Williams approached them. 'Stacey, if you could find the time, Mark and I are having trouble locating the seismograph. The GPS is useless for some unknown reason. Please assist Mark in his search for the seismograph while I take some readings and collect some rock samples near the vents. Lieutenant, you and Ethan can join in the search as well, if you don't mind.'

Spanyer nodded. 'We're happy to help, sir. Come on, Ranger Hardy.'

The four of them spread out in different directions in their search as Williams approached the three, small vented openings that were standing nearly two feet wide. Dr. Stoner, still trying to get a fix on the missing seismograph with the GPS, looked over to where his friend stood, peering into Union Geyser. 'Ben! You're too damn close to those vents. Wait until we get some readings before you stand there.'

Williams scowled. 'I'm well aware of the dangers of hot springs and geysers, Mark, having written quite a few books and research papers on the subject. Besides, as you have already noted, this one has been dormant for nearly sixty years.'

Deep beneath the ground, the earth shifted. A fissure spanning fourteen feet opened, sending an eruption of water and gasses at a temperature of 193 °F upward. Dr. Williams felt the tremor beneath his feet seconds before the eruption engulfed him. The small crater he had been standing beside collapsed, filling immediately with boiling water. A second blast of steam forced Ben Williams' body around, so that he briefly faced his colleagues. He would have been screaming if he weren't already dead. He fell backward into the crater and disappeared. The only sound Ethan heard were the cries of anguish coming from Dr. Stacey Peterson.

NINE

FEDERAL EMERGENCY MANAGEMENT AGENCY, WASHINGTON, D.C.

June 7, 2030.

Fox news ran the report of Dr. Williams' death as its fifth story on the 7:00 P.M. news, after the political, business, financial, and international reports.

'Dr. Benjamin J. Williams, the world-famous scientist and volcanologist, died today due to a tragic accident at Yellowstone National Park, Wyoming. A long-dormant vent he was studying near Shoshone Lake suddenly and without warning erupted, killing him instantly.'

Images of Yellowstone Park played across the screen as the reporter read from his prepared material. A colleague of Dr. Williams at the United States Geological Survey, Denver Federal Office, stated in his interview how much Dr. Williams would be missed and what a brilliant scientist he had been. The entire news report lasted exactly two minutes and eleven seconds. It was little more than a human-interest story.

Administrator Adams sat at his new desk behind those solid mahogany, ten-foot doors and poured himself another shot of scotch whiskey. If he were counting, it was his fifth drink in less than two hours. He replayed the news clip for the eighth time, and just like the previous seven times, the news was the same. His longtime friend and colleague was dead, and he had seen it happen in slow motion last night while he slept, several hours before it actually occurred. In the past, his visions appeared to him weeks or even months before the event took place. It no longer seemed to be the case. If he were correct in his assumption, the time lapse was growing shorter, only a few hours at best. George took another sip from his shot glass and grimaced. His sense of guilt from not warning his friend was overwhelming. There was no way for him to know his vision of Ben's death would happen within a few hours' time, but he still should have attempted to contact him. If he had spoken with Ben before the eruption ... it was doubtful Ben would have heeded the warning. Ben was his friend, but he was also an arrogant son-of-a-bitch. Most likely, he would have asked George if he was hitting the bottle again and hung up the damn phone. *What to do?* Should he inform President Holder that Yellowstone was becoming unstable? Possibly close to an eruption? If he did, he would most likely get the same response that Ben would have given him. He might have been fired from his position at FEMA, too. What proof did he have to offer the White House? *None.* There was no way he could think of to prove his visions were real. It was better to remain quiet. After all, did he really *believe* that he could convince the president of the United States to evacuate the western half of the United States on his word alone?

Administrator Adams let out a mournful sigh of despair and poured himself another large drink.

TEN

SAINT VERAN, FRANCE.

June 25, 2030.

A faint breeze ruffled the bedroom curtains as Clementina Voyant peered out the window. The pitch blackness, save for an occasional flash of lightning, cast strange shadows around the countryside surrounding her family's chateau. According to her father, heavy downpours were forecasted for the night, but the rain had not yet arrived. The cool, damp air gave her goosebumps, and she shivered slightly. Her younger sister, Sophie, was sound asleep in the bed next to hers with her thumb tucked tightly inside her mouth. The peaceful sound of her sister's light breathing was a small comfort to Clem, a nickname her parents had given to her seven years ago at birth. Clem went back to her bed and knelt in silent prayer for the second time. Her prayer was a simple one: a restful night's sleep, free of dreams or nightmares. Climbing back into her bed, she pulled her sheets tightly around her. Sighing, she rolled over and watched her sister for several moments. Clem smiled ruefully. It seemed like forever since she had had a peaceful night's rest. She told her mother and father of the dark dreams she was having every night when they first started close to a year ago, but it was pointless.

'Little Clem,' they had said, 'everyone has bad dreams from time to time. You will outgrow them soon, child.'

The dreams not only continued but had gotten worse. In fact, they were so bad that she would wake up screaming and crying in terror. Clem realized quickly how hollow her parents well-meaning words of comfort had been. The worst night by far was two weeks ago. Her parents heard crying, rushed into her bedroom, and found Clem moaning and thrashing violently in her sleep. When her parents finally woke her from her nightmare, she lied to them when they questioned her.

'I don't remember, Mama,' was her simple reply, but she did remember. She would probably remember what she had dreamt that night for the rest of her life.

* * *

The nightmare had started with her standing on a hillside looking toward the sky. A storm was coming with its dark and menacing clouds. Thunder echoed off the mountains, and it seemed she could even feel the first drops of rain. When she gazed downward, her eyes beheld the crucifixion of Christ. The dream had been so real. It was as if she were there, witnessing His agony. She saw the Roman soldier pierce Jesus with his spear and laugh while blood from the wound ran down His side.

Christ looked directly into her eyes as He spoke the words, 'One day, there will be retribution.'

With that, she was back in France. More horror was there for her to witness. The earth seemed to be on fire; man fed upon man, woman fed upon woman, child fed upon child. The dead were piled high in the streets, and the bodies were bloated with the plague that the rats had once again brought forth. The rats were everywhere she looked, swarming in giant masses that numbered in the millions. They were hungry.

* * *

Clementina pushed her sheets away, got out of bed, and put on her slippers. She tiptoed down the stairs, as if she were in a trance. The chateau was dark and seemed so empty – her parents and the servants had long since retired to bed. She went into her father's library, her favorite room in the mansion, and sat on the cool, marble floor in front of the massive, stone fireplace. Only embers were glowing. She removed the brass poker from its stand and stirred the ashes to life. Staring deeply into the rejuvenated fire, Clem knew there would be no sleep for her on this dark night. She pulled her knees tightly up to her chest as hot tears rolled down her cheeks. Outside, lightning flashed against the distant mountains as rain started to fall.

ELEVEN

DEN HELDER, THE NETHERLANDS.

July 4, 2030.

Diederik Janssen made his way down the craggy, rock cliff
that led to the ocean. The salt spray stung his face and made his
eyes water. Overhead, the sky was growing darker by the minute,
and there wasn't a seagull in sight. Gulls and other sea birds knew
by instinct that trouble was on the way. Listening to the weather
channel on his portable radio for the fifth time this morning, he
looked out over the North Sea. The reports were not good. The
hurricane named *Grace* was out there somewhere. The sea was
calm for the moment, but Diederik had lived all his life along
the coast and knew the weather could change in an instant. The
weather report stated that *Grace* would make landfall sometime
within the next three to four hours. The massive storm had formed
two nights ago, 400 miles out to sea. It was traveling at 35 to
45 miles per hour and measured over 1540 kilometers wide. His
country had never experienced anything like the storm heading
their way. Most of his countrymen and neighbors had moved
further inland, and according to the news, some *the smart ones*
had even left the country all together. That was probably the
sensible thing to do, but he couldn't leave his home; no one,
including himself, considered Diederik Janssen to be a sensible

man. He had sent his wife and their three small children to stay with her parents in Amsterdam less than two hours after the news about *Grace* first broke.

Isabella pleaded with him to accompany them. 'You must come with us, Diederik. If not for your sake, then for the children.'

In the end, though, Isabella had known that her words were useless. Once Diederik made up his mind about something, he never budged from his position. Their goodbyes had been both short and tearful. The children were too young to understand what was happening, but seeing their mother crying got them started, too. He had assured them all he would see them soon and gave each of their wet faces a tender kiss goodbye.

Diederik turned from the sea and made his way quickly back up the path that led to his small home. It was only 9:32 in the morning, but the sky made it appear as though twilight had already fallen.

His neighbor and closest friend, Jager Van Dijk, stood just inside his doorway, waving as he approached. 'Diederik, you have been down to the sea this morning. Tell me, my friend, what is it you have learned?'

'I learned that old men such as you should have gone further inland with your wife.'

Jager gave his longtime friend a mock scowl and laughed out loud. 'If I had left, who would have stayed behind to look after you? Besides, my wife and I need some time apart every once in a while. That is the secret to a long and happy marriage.'

Diederik arched his eyebrows, and his expression was grave. 'This is no time for jokes. The storm heading our way is a serious one. There may still be time for you to leave. The hurricane is not due for another three hours or so.'

Jager gave his friend a sad chuckle. 'I am not going anywhere without you, Diederik. You should know by now after all these years together that I can be just as stubborn as you.' He poured them each a cup of coffee and handed Diederik his cup. 'Besides, our families are safe in Amsterdam, and you need me by your side to keep both of our homes safe.'

Diederik took his mug and tasted the coffee. He grimaced. *Not enough sugar, once again.* 'You are right. I do need you. That much is true. I also know if anything were to happen to your old bones, Ima would never forgive me.'

Jager smiled. 'My Ima loves you like a brother. You know that as well as I do. Stop scolding me as if I were a child and make us some breakfast.'

Diederik gave his friend a warm hug and a kiss on the cheek. 'What would you like me to cook for you this morning since you have volunteered me once again?'

'Sausage and eggs would be nice, along with another mug of my delicious coffee.'

Diederik rolled his eyes at his dear friend. 'Your coffee sucks. I will make us a fresh pot. Something we both can enjoy.'

Jager Van Dijk went to the doorway and peered out. The rain had started to fall in heavy, gray sheets, and the wind was whipping though the trees, causing several of the smaller ones to snap in half. Thick, blackened clouds hung heavy in the sky. 'It looks like your estimate of three hours or so before the storm hits is somewhat inaccurate.'

Diederik walked over and joined Jager by the door. 'The weather stations on the radio this morning said the storm could turn into a Category 5 hurricane. It appears it is too late for either of us to leave. The sausage and eggs are ready. Let's have our breakfast while it's still hot.'

Jager nodded in silence; the two men sat down at the wooden table, bowed their heads, and said a prayer of thanksgiving. After finishing breakfast, Diederik turned his radio back on, only there was nothing but static. Outside, the wind had risen to a maddening, shrieking sound – almost unbearable to hear.

Jager went to the kitchen window, drawn there by the sound of a massive tree falling in the distance. The torrent of rain was so heavy he could barely see more than fifteen feet into the yard. The small house was taking a horrific battering. Another tree was ripped from the ground; with a roar like thunder, it was swept past the window he was standing near and flew out of sight. Jager, his face now white with fear, turned from the window and beckoned for Diederik to join him.

Gale-force winds had created a massive wall of water. As both men stared out the window, they saw it emerge out of the gloomy blackness. Moments later, the window shattered, blinding them both. The torrent of sea water struck the house, crashing through the doors and windows, tearing away the roof. Their dying screams were cut short as both men disappeared beneath the flood waters.

TWELVE

WASHINGTON D.C.

July 4, 2030.

Doug Williams sat behind his desk, tapping his pencil and staring intently at the satellite image in front of him. Hurricane Grace made landfall at approximately 1100 hours on the northernmost tip of the Netherlands and was showing no signs of letting up anytime soon. Reports coming into NOAA stated her sustained windspeeds were measuring in excess of 210 miles per hour, with brief gusts at over 260 miles per hour. The entire coastline was under siege, but the worst damage was to the small town of Den Helder. Satellite photos showed the town to be virtually underwater with only a few rooftops and a church steeple visible. According to the news reports coming out of Holland, many of Den Helder's residents evacuated hours before the storm made landfall, but Williams knew from past experience that some people would have remained behind to look after their property. Those poor souls who stayed were most likely dead, drowned in the floodwaters. *A horrible way to die.* What concerned him, though, was the satellite image he was studying. In his fourth year of working for The National Oceanic and Atmospheric Administration, he spent his entire career studying the weather, and what he was seeing was unfathomable. A second hurricane was forming in the

North Sea at almost the exact originating coordinates of Hurricane Grace. Williams shook his head in disbelief. This new storm system was growing larger by the minute, and it seemed to be on the same course as Grace. Williams wiped the sweat from his hands, picked up his desk phone, and called his supervisor.

* * *

At that precise moment, Administrator Adams was sitting behind his desk, reading the reports and updates concerning Hurricane Grace. The Netherlands was taking a horrific pounding, and he felt both helpless and extremely sad. The vision he had two days ago was replaying in almost exact detail in Holland at the moment, and he had done nothing about it. 'You're a fucking coward,' he whispered under his breath. *What could he have done, though?* Was he supposed to call President Holder and say, 'Sir, I think it would be wise to place a phone call to Prime Minister Hendriksen and let him know that a Category 5 hurricane will be heading his way in a few days and that he needs to evacuate the northern half of his country immediately.'

He could hear the president's response to that news.

'How do you know that, Mr. Adams?'

'Well, sir, several nights ago after I had finished off a pint of my favorite scotch, I had a dream about it.'

Yes, that conversation would have gone over well. A soft knocking on his office door interrupted his thoughts. 'Come in, please.'

His new secretary, Ms. Kate Vetter, entered his office. Regretfully, the lovely Mrs. Samuels retired immediately following the death of Administrator Wright. Ms. Vetter was more than capable in her duties, he thought ruefully, but she didn't have Gloria's legs. 'Yes, Ms. Vetter? What is it? I'm very busy right now.'

'There's a phone call for you on line two, sir.'

'Who is it, Ms. Vetter? I'm really not in the mood to speak with the press.'

'It's Dr. Beverly Anderson, sir. The Administrator of NOAA.'

'I'm well aware of who Dr. Anderson is, Ms. Vetter. I have known her for many years,' he replied, frustrated.

Kate shifted her feet uneasily. 'Yes, sir. I'm sorry.'

George cleared his throat. 'No, Ms. Vetter. I'm the one who should be apologizing. I am very sorry. It has been a long day already, and I have a lot on my mind. Please forgive my rudeness.'

'I understand, sir. No apology is necessary.'

George nodded vaguely. 'If you would be so kind, please bring me a cup of my English tea and some aspirin. I would appreciate it very much.'

'Yes sir. I'll take care of it right away.' With a worried expression on her plain face, she quietly closed the office door behind her.

George sat collecting his thoughts, staring at the blinking red light on his office phone. Beverly was not the kind of person who liked to be kept on hold, but the only reason she would be calling was to relay more bad news. With a growing feeling of apprehension, he picked up the receiver and hit line two. 'Hello, Dr. Anderson. What can I do for you?'

'It's about damn time you picked up the phone, George, and don't give me that *Dr. Anderson* crap. I'm not in the mood. You're not drinking already this morning, are you?'

'Only a cup of weak tea, Beverly. The way you nag me, people would think we were married.'

'Never mind the sarcasm. Have you been paying any attention to what's going on in the Netherlands right now, or does NOAA have to once again bring FEMA up to date?'

George heaved a heavy sigh of frustration. 'I have read all the reports. People are dying in that country. Don't be so fucking flip about it.'

An awkward silence followed his outburst, and for a moment, he wondered if she had hung up the phone.

Then, Beverly responded in a softer voice, 'I'm sorry. You've known me since our college days together at William and Mary. You know I care as much about people as you do, and you also know that the way I deal with situations such as this is with sarcasm. Regardless, I am sorry.'

He took in a deep breath and let it out slowly. 'I know you care, and I am sorry for the way I just spoke to you. What was it that you called to talk with me about?'

She hesitated before continuing, 'There's a new storm system forming in the North Sea right behind Hurricane Grace.'

George swallowed hard. It felt as though all the air was being sucked from his lungs. 'It's not possible, Beverly.'

At her desk in NOAA headquarters, she put the phone down briefly to compose herself and attempt to control her emotions. When she picked up the receiver and spoke again, it was with a strained voice. 'It *is* possible and taking place as we speak. The new system is larger than Hurricane Grace and has already been given a Category 5 classification. She will make landfall sometime within the next five hours.'

He was dumbstruck. 'How fast is this new storm system moving? And what name have you assigned to the second hurricane?'

'According to our deep-space climate observatory, DSCOVR 12, the forward speed is being tracked at just over 70 miles per hour, well above the average of 20 miles per hour.' Beverly paused to let the gravity of that statement settle in. 'We have named her *Grace II* because of her proximity of origin and direction of travel with Hurricane Grace. For all intents and purposes, they are twin sisters.'

George did not respond immediately, but when he did, his voice was barely above a whisper. 'What is being done to evacuate those persons in danger?'

'Damn it to hell, George. Look at your own satellite screen. The entire fucking country is in danger. Over 23 million people live in the Netherlands. There is no air travel at the present time, and there won't be for a week or more. A good portion of the country is already flooded, so there's virtually no way to travel by train or automobile. Do I have to spell it out for you? We are looking at a catastrophe of Biblical proportions when *Grace II* makes landfall, and there's nothing we can do about it. Are you going to place the call to President Holder and inform him of the situation, or do I have to do that for you?'

'I'll make the phone call, Beverly,' George's reply was almost inaudible.

'George, I'm very sorry for the way I just spoke to you. The stress of the job must be getting to me. George, did you hear me?

Are you still on the line?' The only reply she received was the soft click of the phone line going dead.

Administrator Adams looked up from his desk as his office door opened. Ms. Vetter entered carrying a small silver tray with his cup of tea and aspirin on it. 'Thank you very much, Ms. Vetter. Please place a call to the White House for me. I need to speak with President Holder on a matter most urgent.'

Kate gave him a surprised look. 'Yes, sir. If the president's secretary asks what the nature of the urgent matter is, what should I tell her?'

He immediately shot her a look of exasperation, but before he lost his temper again, he calmed himself with a few deep breaths. 'Inform the president's secretary that I need to have a Priority One meeting with the president regarding Hurricane Grace and the Netherlands.

* * *

A young Marine in dress blues silently escorted George into the Oval Office. President Holder was seated behind the Resolute desk and National Security Advisor O'Henry sat to his left on one of the two antique sofas flanking the president's desk. George admired the desk for a quick moment. The desk was a gift from Queen Victoria to President Hayes in 1880. It was made from the timbers of the British exploration ship: HMS Resolute. The Resolute desk was a part of the famous photograph in which John F. Kennedy, Jr. was seen peering out from the panel he had called *The Secret Door.*

'Mr. Adams,' the president began, standing to welcome him into the Oval Office. 'Please take a seat and let us begin. What was your reason for calling a Priority One meeting? My secretary said Ms. Vetter was somewhat vague on the telephone, but it had something to do with the current storm situation in the Netherlands.'

Adams paused for a moment as he took his seat across from O'Henry. 'Yes, sir. As you're aware, Hurricane Grace made landfall at 1100 hours this morning. What you may not be aware of is that a second hurricane has formed at almost the exact same coordinates and, for now, appears to be following the same path as Hurricane Grace.'

President Holder and O'Henry exchanged looks of disbelief. The president regained his composure and said, 'A second hurricane? When did you learn about this, George?'

'I received a phone call from Dr. Beverly Anderson less than 40 minutes ago, sir.'

O'Henry interrupted. 'Excuse me, Mr. Adams. Who is Dr. Beverly Anderson?'

'I'm sorry, sir. Dr. Anderson is the Administrator of NOAA, the National Oceanic and Atmospheric Administration.'

President Holder gazed intently at both men. 'What information can you provide us concerning the new storm system, George?'

'Sir, according to Dr. Anderson, the second hurricane has been dubbed *Grace II* and expected to make landfall at approximately 1600 hours in the same general area of the Netherlands. She is being tracked at a forward speed of 70 miles per hour and has a Category 5 classification.'

Both the president and the national security advisor took in a deep breath. The president stood and began to pace across the American eagle emblazoned on the room's oval carpet. The deceptively small office was silent for several minutes, save for the ticking of a Westminster chime clock sitting on the president's desk.

President Holder paused midstride and faced both men. His expression was grave. 'I need recommendations from both of you, and I need them *now*. There's no time to lose in our response to this catastrophe.'

O'Henry looked doubtful. 'At the moment, our choices are limited, Mr. President. We can't risk any flights into that area with those wind speeds. It would be suicide. Might I suggest you order the carrier group Tripoli, currently stationed in the Mediterranean, to get underway for the North Sea, take up a safe position and await the storms' demise. In the meantime, we can begin preparation to fly in food and medical personnel as soon as the winds die down.'

'Pass those orders along at once, Mr. O'Henry,' Holder said, his voice intensifying. 'And you, Mr. Adams, do you have anything to add to this discussion?'

He swallowed nervously. On the way to the White House, he had made up his mind to tell the president about his visions. But sitting in the Oval Office, his nerve failed him. 'No, sir. I have nothing further to add other than that I concur with what the national security advisor has outlined.'

* * *

George was in a foul mood when he left the Oval Office. His desire for a stiff drink overwhelmed him, but the limousine was only stocked with bottled water. The words he had spoken to the president were stuck on repeat inside his head. 'No, sir. I have nothing further to add other than that I concur with what the national security advisor has outlined.' *That was certainly a helpful response*, he thought sarcastically. As they drove around the National Mall toward FEMA headquarters, George noticed the greenway was crowded with families, lawn chairs, and blankets – anticipation mounting for the 4th of July celebrations. The hotdog and ice cream vendors were in a frenzy, hawking their wares. A small group of children were running and squealing in excitement when their kites lifted high into the sky. Ruefully, he wondered if this would be the last holiday for the United States of America.

Sliding back the privacy window, he said to the driver, 'Let's go down Constitution Avenue and park near the Lincoln Memorial.'

'The traffic will be very heavy heading in that direction, sir.'

'I'm not in any hurry. Please do as I have asked.'

'Yes, sir.'

* * *

Admiring the Lincoln Memorial, Adams took his time trekking up the eighty-seven steps, just as he had done many times in the past. He once again stared into the eyes of the sixteenth president sitting immortalized in marble before him. President

Abraham Lincoln had been a brave man, a man of integrity and compassion. *I am a drunken coward. I was given this power to foresee future events for a reason. The gift was certainly not bestowed upon me to keep the information to myself. If there is a God in Heaven, he should have chosen a better messenger than me.* George tore his eyes away from the statue and quickly made his way back down the steps.

***

Arriving back at his office, Ms. Vetter greeted him with an admonishing *where have you been?* look but stopped when she saw the distress clouding his face.

'Yes, Ms. Vetter. What is it?'

'I called the White House, sir. The president's secretary said that you left over two hours ago.'

'I was not aware I had to check in with you and keep you posted concerning my whereabouts.'

'It's not that, sir, but Dr. Anderson has called several times to speak with you. She sounded most urgent.'

'Please place a phone call to her office and inform her that I am back.'

'Yes, sir. I'll take care of it right now.'

'Wait. I'll make the phone call, myself.'

Nodding in response, she excused herself from his office and closed the door.

George slumped into his overstuffed leather chair and stared at the phone as though it were an adversary. *What the hell could Beverly want now?* Unlocking his bottom desk drawer, he took out a bottle of scotch and squeezed it. In the dim light cast by his desk lamp, he stole a quick glance around his office to see if there was anyone to bear witness to his weakness. No one was hiding in the shadows, preparing to jump out and catch him the moment the bottle touched his lips. Acting like a schoolboy who had been caught cheating on an exam, he returned the bottle to its hiding place without touching a drop and dialed Beverly's office. She picked up on the first ring.

'George, did you speak with the president?'

'Hello to you, Beverly. I did speak directly with the president and the national security advisor.'

'Their response?'

'Mr. O'Henry has advised the president to have Tripoli make for the North Sea and wait until it's reasonably safe to assist in rescue operations. In addition, the president has ordered transport planes be put on standby with food, water, and medical supplies – taking off as soon as the winds die down, and it's safe to fly.'

'That's it? That's all they are going to do?'

'What else can they do, Beverly? If they order those transport planes into that windstorm, they will be torn to pieces. And if the carrier group gets too close to the hurricanes, those ships would be tossed around like toy boats.'

'I'm sorry, George. You're right. I guess I was hopeful for a more immediate response.'

'I know, but everything that can be done is being done. Any further news regarding Grace II?'

Beverly swallowed hard before answering. 'Yes. Grace II made landfall shortly after 4:00 P.M. near the town of Callantsoog, roughly twenty miles from Den Helder. We have received reports from the International Space Station Venture I that the two hurricanes have merged into one, with a gale diameter measuring over 1920 kilometers. We have confirmed reports that waves with the tsunami classification of over 70 feet high are hitting at regular intervals along the entire coastline of Holland. Hurricane Grace had already breached many of the dikes located throughout the countryside, and the two main rivers, Rhine and Meuse, overflowed several hours ago. With the two merged hurricane systems, all of the Netherlands will experience massive flooding to some degree.'

'Is there any word on the death toll?'

'No, George. We have not received any word concerning casualties at this point in time, but we both know the number will be in the hundreds, if not the thousands.'

George rocked slowly back in his chair and stared at the ceiling. 'I think we both know by now that you're being overly optimistic. You were right when you stated a catastrophe of Biblical proportions. Righter than you know,' he whispered.

Beverly cleared her throat nervously. 'What do you mean by that remark? What are you saying?'

'Nothing. If the death toll is below the 100,000 mark, I'll be very surprised. For that matter, I think we will both be surprised.'

'My God. I pray you are wrong.'

'So, do I, Beverly.'

After he hung up, George stood up from his desk and locked his office door. Turning off his table lamp, the only sound in the pitch-black room was the bottom drawer being opened. He sat down on the hardwood floor and put the bottle to his lips. *So, do I, Beverly.*

His heart and mind knew the truth – *saw* the truth. The dead and dying would be piled high once the hurricane had finished God's work. One hundred thousand dead would only be the beginning ... of the end.

THIRTEEN

CAMINO DE SANTIAGO, SPAIN.

July 21, 2030.

In the spring of 1945, the Russian army invaded Berlin, Germany, and Eberhardt Hoffmann had been conceived in the most brutal manner imaginable. In a lust for vengeance, Russian soldiers raped over 100,000 women and young girls in Berlin, alone. Eberhardt's mother, a young girl of fourteen, had been one of them. While Adolf Hitler and his bride, Eva Braun, were committing suicide deep inside the subterranean Führerbunker by way of cyanide poisoning and bullet, his future mother was being gang raped and beaten by a group of five members of the Russian army.

He knew all the details of what happened to his mother on that April morning because his grandmother witnessed the horrific assault from her bedroom closet, where she remained hidden while holding her own infant son tightly to her chest. His grandmother recounted the entire story on his seventh birthday and left no detail of the assault untold. It seemed as if his grandmother wanted him to commit it to memory for all time, and that was exactly what Eberhardt had done. The soldiers had each taken his mother multiple times on that April morning, laughing at her while she laid bleeding on the dirt floor and begging for their mercy. Once the soldiers' carnal desires were satisfied, they beat her out of revenge for the war crimes the German army had committed against Mother Russia. Two months after his birth, his mother hung herself from a wooden crossbeam in her small bedroom. Eberhardt was in his crib and the only witness to her sin as she put the rope around her neck and tightened it. He always wondered if she kissed him goodbye.

Less than a week after his seventh birthday, his grandmother took both his eight-year-old uncle and him to a monastery in Spain for orphaned children of the war. Built into the ancient stone wall surrounding the monastery were two solid brass doors: one large enough for a child to walk through and the other where infants could be left in a simple wooden cradle. The monks had no contact with the outside world; once a child or infant was left to their care, there was no turning back. His grandmother had waited for him to reach an age where he would have understood what happened to his mother before taking her own son and him to the orphanage. His grandmother, having lived with her guilt and shame for the past eight years over not protecting her daughter from the Russian soldiers, hung herself from an oak tree less than twenty paces from the monastery's moss-covered stone walls.

* * *

Eberhardt sat by his bedroom window, studying the old oak tree. He had memorized all its leaves and branches, but even at the age of eighty-four, he always wondered which branch she hung herself from. He became a monk and taken a vow of silence on his nineteenth birthday, twelve years and six days after stepping foot inside the monastery walls for the first and last time. It was rumored the oak tree he was staring at had been planted the same year the last stone was added to the monastery walls over 422 years ago. At the age of nine, he made inquiries concerning his family history. He learned his uncle died of pneumonia within weeks of their arrival at the monastery and was buried in the small crypt beneath the monastery's church. There was no other known information, except of his grandmother who had committed the unforgivable sin of taking her own life. When he asked for more details, he was told of the hanging from the oak tree; she had been cremated – her ashes were scattered with the wind – as she was not deemed worthy of a Christian burial.

He rose slowly from his chair and shuffled to the simple table next to his bed where his tattered Bible rested. With great care, he opened the holy book to one of his favorite verses, John 8:7, and read it. *Let the one among you who is without sin be the first to cast a stone at her.* He went back to his chair and once again gazed down at the ancient oak tree. *Yes, it was true that his grandmother had committed a grave sin by taking her own life, but who among us is without sin?* Eberhardt knew that his thoughts were heresy, but he had spent his entire life in silent study of the Bible and its teachings. If a sinful man could not attain everlasting life in Heaven, then Heaven must be a lonely place. It was true Jesus Christ died on the cross for the sins of mankind, but it was also true that Christ's last words spoken on the cross detailed eventual retribution for the sinful. He knew this the same way that the young French girl did. He, Eberhardt Hoffmann, had stood on that same windswept hillside as the young girl. And he, Eberhardt Hoffmann, was also cursed and blessed with the visions of the end of days that would soon take place by fire, water, and plague.

He fell to his knees and began to pray. Ever since his seventh birthday when his dear grandmother had told him of the horrors his mother endured at the hands of those evil men, his heart and soul were filled with a burning hatred for all mankind. He prayed feverishly for the fire, the water, and the plague that the rats and the birds would carry to every corner of the planet – for the damnation and eternal punishment of all men.

FOURTEEN

BARRIÈRE D'ENFER (GATE OF HELL), PARIS, FRANCE.

July 25, 2030.

His namesake was Benoit Fontaine, but he was now known simply as Benny. Long ago, his mother smiled proudly when she told him his name meant *blessed*. If it had ever been true, it certainly no longer was. He was anything but blessed; regardless, it was a pleasant memory for a man who had so few fond thoughts to keep him company. He had been respectable at one time: a man of means with a small amount of wealth and fine clothing ... a man who ordered the finest of foods in any restaurant. The only restaurant catering to his wishes these days was the dirty soup kitchen in the poorest section of town. He was one of the thousands of homeless individuals who called the streets and sewers of Paris his home. His home address was a park bench or an alleyway filled with the refuse of mankind. His bed was made of old discarded newspapers, keeping him warm when he lay down for the night. He was a man with no hope ...

Last night, near midnight, he had been lucky – a rare occurrence at this late stage of life. While out on a twilight search for anything of value, he had found a small change purse filled with several coins laying in the street. He tossed the purse, minus the coins, into the trash, lest he get caught with it by the police and accused of theft. Instead of week-old stale bread covered in mold this morning, he would feast on fresh bread and a cup of café noir while his tiny four-legged friend, a small Yorkshire Terrier named Sam, dined on a soup bone.

Sam was sound asleep, snoring softly by his side. Half-kneeling, Benny pushed aside his tattered blanket and collection of newspapers. He scanned the alley, but there was nothing to see except garbage cans, trash, old boxes, and stacked crates. He had chosen his spot with care and was pleased to have not been molested during the night by either other roving homeless thieves looking for anything of value or the police patrols who might have taken him to jail for vagrancy. He grabbed his walking stick and stood up with great care. Gently prodding Sam with the end of his stick, the dog woke at once and gave him a baleful look of annoyance in return.

'Come on, boy. Get up. Let's get this day started.'

Sam yawned, rolled over, and curled further under the blanket. Benny gave the small dog another prod with the stick, and Sam stretched in reluctance. The morning sun was already at its summit and held the promise of another warm, muggy day as man and dog made their way out of the alley and onto Denfert-Rochereau Street. In front of him were the stone archways of the Barrière d'Enfer, better known to the English tourists as the Gate of Hell. Every homeless person he knew avoided this area because of a superstitious dread of the dead buried in the nearby Catacombes de Paris – the final resting place for more than six million people. The thought that his fellow streetwalkers were still afraid of ghosts made him smile. Sam wandered off toward the catacombs' entrance to relieve himself in the bushes.

* * *

Deep underground in the world's largest gravesite, the first rat to catch the small dog's scent lifted its nose and tested the air. It was slightly larger than the terrier's eleven pounds and dark brown in color with a tail that extended close to ten inches in length. Ravenously hungry, its nose located the small dog's location immediately. Salivating, the rat emitted a low vocalization, and within moments, it was joined by dozens more of its kind. What they all had in common: their unusually large size, voracious appetite, and infestation of fleas. Thousands of fleas swarmed their shiny dark hair, carrying a new strain of the Bubonic Plague that had never been experienced by mankind. A new variant of the Black Death was about to make its first appearance and claim its first victim.

* * *

Sam picked up the rat's scent less than two minutes after the large brown rodent had picked up his ... a minute too late. A massive black female rat was the first to attack, biting the dog's rear leg and ripping the tendon nearly in half. He let out a loud yelp of pain and terror. Benny, dumbfounded by the cry, looked up from the trashcan he had been rummaging through. At the same moment, a second rat tore out the small terrier's throat. Before Benny could react, the dog was dead, and his body was being dragged below into the catacombs. Without hesitation, Benny hobbled into the darkness, hoping to rescue his one true friend in this world. It was his last mistake in a lifetime full of mistakes. Hundreds of rats attempting to eat the small terrier, turned as one to face the intruder. Their razor-sharp teeth clicked. As he turned to run, they had already flanked him. There was no escape. His desperate scream was cut short as the swarm descended upon him. While they feasted on his body, millions of other flea-infested rats spread throughout the sewers of Paris, France, and Europe. All the rats were hungry, but for now, they waited patiently. It was not their time, yet. Soon. The Black Death that resulted in the deaths of 75 to 200 million people across Europe and central Asia between 1348 and 1666 A.D. would be insignificant compared to what was about to take place ...

* * *

On the outskirts of Saint Veran, 458 miles away, a young girl of seven woke from her nightmare. Her screams filled the chateau.

FIFTEEN

THE WHITE HOUSE, WASHINGTON, D.C.

July 27, 2030. 1:50 P.M.

It had been twenty-three days since the twin hurricanes struck the Netherlands, leaving behind in their wake a path of death and destruction by a force of nature never witnessed before in human history. President Holder stood next to an antique eighteenth-century globe, a gift from the people of England during his first year in office. With his arms folded across his chest, he gazed thoughtfully out the south window onto the green manicured lawn below him. Seated behind him on the two leather-bound sofas flanking his desk were Chief of Naval Operations Admiral James Stockton, Vice President Timmons, and National Security Advisor O'Henry. Coffee, tea, and assorted pastries sat untouched on the table in front of them. The mood in the room was ominous. President Holder, known throughout Washington, D.C. as a genial host, had barely spoken one word to the three men in the Oval Office in forty-five minutes. A soft knocking on the northwest door that opened into the main corridor of the West Wing roused the president from his thoughts. He turned from the window with an audible sigh and crossed over the thick carpet to answer the door.

A Secret Service agent was standing ramrod straight in front of him. 'I have Administrator Adams with me, sir. Do you wish to see him at this time?'

President Holder's face tightened for a moment before he let out a slow breath. 'Yes. Show him in.'

George entered the Oval Office with a feeling of dread. His head was pounding from the stressors of his job, and his mouth felt like it had been stuffed with cotton. Most of all, he had not requested this meeting with the president. Rather, the president had requested this meeting with him.

President Holder returned to the window, ignoring George for the moment. His hand touched various points on the globe next to him, studying it for several minutes. When he spoke, it was barely audible. 'Please take a seat, George, and help yourself to the coffee.'

He gazed at the president's back. 'Thank you, sir.' *There's something wrong here.* He sat down next to William O'Henry and poured himself a cup of tea. As he did so, he did not make eye contact with any of the men in the room.

President Holder turned to face the men he had summoned to the White House. 'First, I would like to thank each one of you for coming to the White House on such short notice. I know how busy your schedules are.' Taking his seat, he picked up several papers that had been arranged in a neat row on his desk, glanced briefly at them with a somber expression on his face, and then laid them back down. After a few silent and uncomfortable minutes, he surveyed the men seated before him. Speaking in a slow, measured voice, he said, 'George, I would like for you to update us on the situation in the Netherlands.'

George shifted uneasily on the sofa and cleared his throat. 'Mr. President, the news is all bad, I'm sorry to report. Much of the country remains flooded and inaccessible. Based upon aerial and satellite photos, it appears the country may remain that way for quite some time.'

Vice President Timmons leaned forward, his expression grave. 'Why is that, Mr. Adams?'

George studied the vice president. It was quite clear Timmons did not like him. 'The flood waters are not receding, sir. Torrential rains followed the two hurricanes almost immediately, and as of this morning, the rains have not abated.'

The vice president gave a short grunt of acknowledgement, reclined back on the sofa, and folded his hands on his lap.

President Holder reached for his favorite pipe and put it into his mouth without lighting it. With a pained expression on his face, he asked, 'What word do you have on casualties, George?'

He looked directly into the president's eyes. 'The death toll will be staggering, sir. Early estimates from our Navy, and I am sure Admiral Stockton will concur, put the count at well over 120,000 dead and an untold number injured. What word we have been supplied with from the Netherlands' government puts the numbers at roughly the same amount.' He paused for a moment to let the gravity of his last statement settle in. 'As of today, twenty-three days after the hurricanes made landfall, there are still hundreds of dead bodies floating in the flood waters.'

President Holder sat back hard in his chair, a look of disbelief etched on his face. Turning toward Admiral Stockton, he asked, 'Is this true, James?'

Admiral Stockton gave a grim nod. 'I'm afraid it is true, Mr. President. In the Navy's defense, sir, the carrier group Tripoli has been working around the clock. My office has received several reports of serious accidents, including the deaths of two of our pilots being blamed on exhaustion. I repeat, we are doing all we can with the available resources. If you wish, sir, you could order another group into the area, but that would leave us rather thin in the Atlantic Ocean.'

Sitting at his desk, the president felt the weight of his office bearing down upon him. The reports sitting in front of him were Top Secret; they were meant for the eyes of the President of the United States only. For this reason, President Holder had not yet disclosed their contents to any of the four men sitting before him. If what was contained within the reports were ever made public, it would start a worldwide panic on a scale never seen. The first report had been delivered in-person early yesterday by the most noted volcanologist alive. The second report was from the American Embassy in China, which had been hand-delivered this morning by the personal envoy of Ambassador James Barnell.

The report stated hundreds of cases of a contagious bacterial disease had been isolated in several hospitals in the region of Inner Mongolia and the provinces of Heilongjiang and Liaoning. According to Ambassador Barnell, there were now 522 confirmed deaths with fear the number would climb much higher. The Chinese government, whose internal policy had always been to remain as secretive as possible, refused to confirm these reports. China was making every effort to keep this information from the public. There was the very real possibility that China might be facing a new, never-before-seen potential outbreak of the plague. President Holder was a man who liked to handle one problem at a time, but as president, that was a luxury he could ill afford, especially at this crucial time. President Holder stood purposefully and turned his rigid gaze to Admiral Stockton. 'James, I want you to give the order for a second carrier group to get under way for the Netherlands and render all assistance necessary to carrier group Tripoli. Please see to it at once.'

As Admiral Stockton left the Oval Office to carry out his orders, President Holder turned to Timmons and O'Henry. 'If you both would be so kind, I would like to have a private conversation with Administrator Adams.'

Timmons rose to his feet with a look of annoyance and left the Oval Office, followed closely by O'Henry. When the door closed behind them, President Holder took a seat next to George on the sofa and poured himself a cup of coffee. 'George, what I am about to tell you is top secret and not to be discussed with anyone. But first, I need you to answer a direct question.'

He studied the president's face and simply replied, 'Yes, sir. Of course.'

'You said back on April 18th, and I quote from my notes during the meeting, that you were of the belief we may be facing a period of global weather change and strongly feared the storms would not only continue but get much worse. Do you remember making that statement?'

The words the president had just spoken hung in the air between the two men. George suddenly felt hollow inside. 'Yes, sir. I remember making that statement.'

With an uncharacteristic bluntness in his voice, President Holder looked deep into George's eyes and asked, 'Why did you say that?'

He averted his eyes from those of the president's. 'I would rather not comment on that, Mr. President.'

'Listen to me carefully, George. I will not accept that answer, so I'll ask you again. Why did you make that statement?'

He turned his head slowly to face the most powerful man on the planet. The moment he had been dreading for so long had finally arrived, and he felt some small measure of relief to confess. 'I can foresee these storms before they take place, sir. I have had this gift since I was a young boy. My grandmother was also blessed with divination. I know it sounds unbelievable, even crazy, but it is the truth.'

President Holder looked incredulous momentarily at what he had just heard. When it passed, his expression softened. 'I'm not willing to admit I believe you, George, but I will remain open-minded to the possibility that what you have told me is the truth. For what it's worth, I do believe that you think you are being truthful. Right now, we have more important issues to discuss.'

Stunned, George felt relieved. He had not been dismissed on the spot as he had been expecting.

The president stood up from the sofa, walked to his desk, and exhaled in despair. Turning, he faced George once again. 'As I mentioned before, these papers are top secret. For that matter, they are marked for my eyes only. After I inform you of their contents, you and I will be two of only three men in the United States with this knowledge.'

George arched his eyebrows. A feeling of unease was coming over him. 'May I know the identity of the third man, sir?'

'Of course, George. His name is Dr. Mark Stoner.'

* * *

George let the president's words sink in. 'Dr. Stoner is aware of what is contained in this top-secret report, sir?'

President Holder nodded. 'He should be, George. He is the one who wrote the report and hand-delivered it to me yesterday morning. As I understand it, you two are close friends.'

He gave a wan nod. 'Yes, sir. We are close. But I had no idea that you were friends with him, too.'

'I have few friends, and I am not one to use the terms *friend* or *friendship* lightly. Let us just say that Mark and I are on a first name basis and have known each other for many years. I am sure you are aware Dr. Stoner was conducting tests at Yellowstone National Park on June 7th when the tragic death of Dr. Ben Williams occurred.'

'Yes, sir. I am aware of that. Ben was a close friend of mine, too. It was on my recommendation that both Ben and Mark conduct tests at Yellowstone. In a way, I am responsible for Ben's death.'

The president rose from his seat, approached George, and placed his hand gently on his shoulder. He wasn't very good at providing comfort during such difficult times because he felt words seemed insignificant when a loved one or close friend died. 'It wasn't your fault, George. There was no way for you to have known what was going to happen on that day.'

He glanced up at the president, feeling somewhat ashamed for having become emotional in the Oval Office of all places. 'Thank you, sir. I appreciate your words of comfort more than you know.'

The president smiled warmly at him. 'If you're ready, I would like to discuss both reports with you. I need your opinion and advice, and for some reason, I feel time is not on our side.'

The dark feeling of dread returned like a shroud being pulled over his head, but George replied with a simple, 'Yes, sir. I am ready to hear those reports.' He wondered sadly if he would soon regret that statement.

The president returned to his desk and sat down heavily, like a man with a huge burden on his back because of way too many responsibilities. He opened the first report, which George assumed to be Dr. Stoner's. 'George, this first report is Dr. Stoner's. It states he fears the volcano under Yellowstone may be unstable.' He handed over the small black binder with the words Top Secret printed in bold red letters on its cover. 'His premises supporting this conclusion are listed on this section of his report.'

George read the report slowly, taking every word into account:

(1) Multiple seismometers located throughout Yellowstone National Park show a dramatic increase in seismic activity.

(2) Seismic data shows both minor and major earthquakes are migrating toward the surface. This may suggest magma is also migrating toward ground level.

(3) Substantial ground deformations have been measured at multiple locations with some bulges being measured at three to four meters. Resurgent domes also being reported where none had existed in the past.

(4) Monitored gasses from multiple fumaroles show a substantial anomalous increase in temperature. This may suggest magma is moving closer to the surface.

(5) Multiple signs of tree and plant life dying in areas where known vents are located.

(6) Multiple lakes and ponds have changed to a copper color. pH readings show a low reading of 1.0, and in some cases 0.0, indicating a much higher than normal acidic level.

(7) There is a new development of a lava lake which has created a massive depression near Grand Prismatic Spring and Mallard Lake Dome.

(8) An increase in rumbling noises being reported by both the National Park Service and tourists.

George placed the report back on the desk in front of him and poured himself another cup of tea. He desperately wished he had some brandy to go with it. The report he had just read was damning evidence that an eruption of some form was preparing to take place. Whether or not it would be a massive super eruption or something on a much smaller scale, no one could say at this time, but right now, the president of the United States was looking to him for some answers.

Leaning forward in his chair with his hands clasped, he said, 'George, please tell me what you are thinking.'

'Before I answer your question, sir, could you tell me what Dr. Stoner's hypothesis is?'

President Holder stared hard at George for what seemed like an eternity. 'I could, but I won't. I want to hear what you have to say independent of Dr. Stoner's report.'

George swallowed to clear his throat. 'I think we should begin preparations for an eruption, sir. On what scale that eruption might be, no one can say at this time.'

The president jumped to his feet and glared down at him with a hardened expression. 'That's bullshit, George. I think you know what's going to happen, and I want the answer *now*. You just finished telling me you had this gift of *foresight*, as you referred to it.'

George grimaced for a moment, but sadness clouded his features. 'It doesn't work that way, Mr. President. I can't control what I see or when I see it. I don't foresee every major storm or natural disaster that takes place. Yellowstone could erupt tomorrow or next week, and I might see it happen in a dream the night before or not at all. I'm sorry.'

President Holder returned to his seat. His face was flushed. 'I'll tell you what Mark believes will happen.' He picked up a single sheet of notepaper from his desk and read it aloud. 'In conclusion, it is my belief that if an eruption does take place in the near future at Yellowstone National Park, it will be a major one, extending far beyond the boundaries of the state of Wyoming.' Returning the paper to his desk, he frowned at the man sitting across from him. 'What the hell am I supposed to do with this information, George?'

'I don't know, sir. Perhaps an evacuation plan should be put in place for Wyoming.'

'An evacuation of Wyoming? There are over 650,000 people living in that state, and your advice to me is to evacuate them? Do you have any idea of the panic that would ensue if I issued an evacuation order to that many people? What if you and Dr. Stoner are wrong? What if Yellowstone is stable? I need concrete answers before I order an evacuation of that magnitude. I also want your estimation of what would take place in Wyoming and its border states if a super eruption were to take place.'

George glanced up at the president of the United States. There was a deep sorrow in his eyes and an odd smile formed with his mouth. 'If Yellowstone has a super eruption, sir, you will not have to worry about the state of Wyoming any longer. It is my belief that every state west of Missouri would cease to exist within moments, and the eruption of Mount St. Helens would seem like a firecracker by comparison. The rest of the United States would have an ash cloud form above it, raining down ash and pumice for months, if not years. Crops would die, and widespread famine would kill a majority of the survivors. Then, the entire planet would face what is called a *nuclear winter*. Mankind would cease to exist, Mr. President. So, no. I would not worry about Wyoming very much, sir."

SIXTEEN

MANHATTAN, NEW YORK CITY, NEW YORK.

August 4, 2030. 2:05 P.M.

'Let's go back to March 18th and start this afternoon's session from there, Robert.'

'You have heard me talk about that incident more times than I care to remember, Dr. Fleming. Do I really have to go over that day with you, again?'

'Your superiors at the police department want a report on your progress, Robert, and we both know your emotional problems started on that day. So, yes, we do need to discuss it once again. Not to mention, I have received several phone calls from your supervisors at the N.Y.P.D. over concerns you seem to be depressed lately.'

Robert exhaled in frustration and jumped up from the couch. 'Who the hell has been calling you behind my back, this fucking time?'

Dr. Fleming fidgeted nervously. The enormous man pacing back and forth in his office was clearly agitated. 'You know from our past sessions that I cannot reveal any names to you. Where I get my information is not your concern. You also know I frown upon the use of profanities in my presence. Please return to your seat so that we can begin this session. Our time is very limited.'

He gazed down at the doctor, displaying his heightened frustration. 'You psychiatrists are all the same. You act like you give a damn about your patients, but you keep one eye on the clock and the other eye on your reception room, waiting for your next dollar to walk into the office. You tell me not to use profanities in front of you; yet, I don't know how many times I have had to ask you not to claim that I have *emotional problems*. You make me sound like some fucking nutjob.'

From past experience, the doctor knew it was best to remain quiet when a patient was having an emotional outburst. Robert returned to his seat during the awkward silence and stared at him, waiting for a response. 'I am very sorry. I know you have asked me in the past not to use the phrasing: *emotional problems*. By way of explanation, it's the terminology psychiatrists use in our course of work. Shall we begin with our session?'

Exasperated, he gave a casual shrug. 'Sure, Doc. Whatever the hell you say.'

* * *

I was laying there on my deathbed, only my deathbed was a dirty floor and I was hog-tied, face-down in the filth. My wrists were tied to my ankles, good and tight.'

'What were your thoughts at that exact moment, Robert? What were you feeling?'

'I was thinking: I am about to die while all around the world people are going about their daily lives. Outside of this crappy store, people are walking by on the sidewalk, enjoying the day without a care. My wife and three-year-old daughter are at home playing with toys or watching a cartoon on TV. People are on vacation. People are having sex. People are enjoying a steak dinner. I'm on a dirty floor. I'm about to be shot in the back of my head. Wrong place, wrong-fucking-time.'

'Glancing at his notes, the doctor said, 'Since your last visit in July, have you had any contact with your wife or daughter?'

'My *ex-wife* is what you meant to say, Doc. And the answer is still no, just like every other time that you have asked me that damn question. You know that she moved with my daughter to

California to live with her sister three years ago. She divorced me and took my daughter away five months after I walked in on that armed robbery. Guess she didn't want to be married to a coward.'

'Is that how you feel about yourself, Robert? That you are a coward?'

He closed his eyes and rubbed his forehead. 'Yes, Doc. That's exactly the way I feel, and every minute since that day.'

He closed his notebook quietly and looked into Robert's eyes. 'There was nothing you could have done that afternoon. Nothing. There was a gun pointed at your forehead and another gun pressed against your back. I repeat, there was nothing you or anyone else could have done at that moment.'

Robert shot the doctor an angry look. 'You're wrong. You're more wrong than you could ever know. I could have been a man. A Marine. A police officer. I should have done something, *anything*. Even if it had meant my death. Life is pointless ... meaningless. I could have been murdered that day, and if I had been, what would have been the point of my life? What was the point of high school or college? The Marines? Or the police academy? Is that what people who are dying of old age or cancer feel like in their final moments?'

Shifting uneasily in his chair, he stated, "I don't think so, Robert. Every life has its purpose. You have never spoken about your feelings this way before. Why now? What has changed?'

He did not respond at first, but with tears in his eyes, he looked up. 'I don't want to go there, Doc.'

'You have to, Robert. It would be good for you to let it out.'

He felt his mind reeling back to that March afternoon. Then, he blurted it out. 'I hated everyone at that moment. *Everyone.* I still feel that way today. That's why my wife took my daughter and left me. She could see what I was becoming, see the hate in my eyes, and she didn't want to subject our daughter to what was eating away at me.'

'I need to ask you one more question before I let you leave today. It is imperative that you are honest with me.'

He wiped his eyes as he tried to compose himself. 'Sure, Doc. What is it that you want to know now?'

'Do you ever think about suicide? Does that thought ever cross your mind?'

He had been a cop for more than twenty-six years. He knew enough about body language and eye contact to get away with telling a lie. He also knew that if he told the truth he might as well go back to police headquarters and turn in his gun and badge. He looked the doctor straight in the eye. 'No, Dr. Fleming. It's not something I ever think about.'

* * *

Leaving the office, Gray walked past an attractive woman sitting in the waiting room. Their eyes met briefly, and she offered him a shy smile that was not reciprocated. He wanted to grab her by the shoulders, tell her to forget about her appointment, and to leave the office at once. He wanted to tell her to get on with her life and enjoy what little time was left for her and everyone else on this miserable planet. He slowly closed the office door behind him with an inaudible click. As he got on the elevator, he pondered the doctor's last question. Why should he commit suicide now? There was no longer any need for him to think about doing it. Judgement Day was merely a few short months away or even sooner: fire, water, and plague. There was no need for him to take his hidden stash of pills to end his life. Everyone was going to die very soon. Even the good Dr. Clayton Fleming. That thought brought a rare smile to his face.

SEVENTEEN

VATICAN CITY, ROME, ITALY.

August 21, 2030. 2:27 P.M.

Knees cracking as he rose from his office chair, Cardinal Borgogni slid his Bible into his desk's top drawer and walked into his bedchamber through a doorway hidden behind an eighteenth-century tapestry woven with a depiction of Michelangelo Buonarroti's masterpiece, *The Last Judgement*. Kneeling next to his bedside, he smoothed out his simple, white cassock and began his afternoon prayer.

'Keep your promise, Lord, and forgive my sins, for they are many. Those who have reverence for the Lord will learn from him the path they should follow.'

The prayer was not for himself – he was sure that the Kingdom of Heaven would be open to him – it was for the billions of souls at risk of eternal damnation as Judgement Day approached. The Lord, Our Father, was preparing a cruel punishment for the human race, and few would be spared his wrath. Whispers within the Vatican hallways and behind closed doors, from those who were aware, thought the imminent judgement was too harsh. He was not one of them: who was he to question God's will?

While he was finishing his prayers for mercy and divine guidance, a small silver bell tinkled beside him, indicating the

Swiss Guard was standing outside his office door with Father Joseph. He got to his feet with great difficulty; his back and legs hurt often these days. Crossing the room, he opened the door to find the father standing in a position of respect with his head bowed low and his hands clasped together at his waist. The cardinal dismissed the Swiss Guardsman with a slight wave of his hand.

'Come in, Joseph, and please sit down. We have ...,' Cardinal Borgogni hesitated, '... something unfortunate to discuss.'

'Thank you, Eminence.' Father Joseph stole a glance at Cardinal Borgogni as he entered the office and took his seat. He had already reported to the cardinal this morning regarding Sister Adelina and Father Francis; it was most unusual for him to be summoned back.

The cardinal sat down across from him and paused before speaking. 'I have unpleasant news to share with you.'

With a slight nod of his head, he said, 'Yes, Eminence?'

Leaning forward, the cardinal placed both of his hands on Joseph's shoulders. 'Father Francis has been called home to Heaven, my son. It happened a few hours after your visit with him this morning. The Swiss Guard stationed outside of his door heard a chair fall over. When they received no response to their inquiry, they entered his bedchamber and found him lying dead on the floor. I am very sorry, Joseph.'

In a state of shock, he sat very still in his chair until he found his voice. 'He seemed so well this morning. He spoke of his garden and his tomatoes. How could this happen?'

Shoulders drooping slightly, the cardinal said, 'Father Francis was very old. Let us leave it there, my son. It is not our place to question God's will, and we have other ...,' he paused, '... more urgent matters to discuss.'

Shifting in his seat, he wiped his eyes with a handkerchief. 'Other matters, Eminence?'

'Yes, Joseph. There are certain facts that must be revealed to you now that Father Francis has passed, and time is growing short. First, you should know I have been visiting with Father Francis twice-daily for many years to provide a comparison of revealings. Do not take it personally, but Father Francis was much more forthright with me than with you. I believe he felt he needed to protect you in some way from his darker visions.'

Father Joseph interrupted. 'And what was it that he revealed to you, Eminence, that he would not reveal to me?'

'He revealed the complete truth to me, Joseph. A truth most men, even those of us in the clergy, would have a hard time comprehending. The truth is that God's Judgement Day is upon us, and it will be a harsh judgement; however, not even Father Francis knew the exact timing of the end of days. What we do know is that it will be soon – the signs are very clear. The next thing you must know concerns the individual we have referred to as Sister Adelina.'

'Sister Adelina?' He swallowed nervously, his mind reeling.

'Please, Joseph. No more interruptions. Sister Adelina Bonomo died at an extremely old age on November 10, 1941, and left no family behind. The individual you have visited with all these years was simply a name given to a woman as a means of personal reference. Father Francis was a soldier for Christ and a devout servant of the church. Unfortunately, the same cannot be said of the one we refer to as Sister Adelina. We believe the woman, *this imp*, to be a servant of evil: an ungodly creature – Satan's representative here on Earth. What her purpose is, no one can say. Three days following the death of the true Sister Adelina, she was found wandering the streets of Rome by the police and brought to a nearby hospital for care. During her stay at the hospital, her behavior became more and more violent, requiring restraint. On one occasion, a nurse reported that she spoke in the voice of an old man in a language no one recognized. From that point forward, none of the hospital staff would enter her room to provide her with care. The hospital records listed her age at the time she was brought to the hospital to be approximately thirty years old. This was only a guess, of course. If she were thirty years old in 1941, then her age right now would be somewhere around 120. She was brought to the Vatican hospital, where it was determined the language she was speaking was Aramaic: the common language of Judea from the first century AD and primary language of Jesus and His disciples. Father James was the creature's caretaker over forty-seven years ago, long before your arrival here at the Vatican. One day, Father James was tricked by this imp into making contact. How? We do not know. Suffice it to say, he died a raving madman three days later without ever speaking another word – why you were commanded to never allow yourself to be touched by her. I am sure that you have many questions for me, Joseph. You may ask them now.'

Dumbfounded by what he had heard, a terrible pain formed in his forehead and nausea overwhelmed him. 'I am uncertain where to begin, Eminence, but I have a difficult time believing this woman is almost 120 years old. May I ask what Aramaic words she spoke?'

Cardinal Borgogni raised his eyebrows, and his expression hardened. 'Father Joseph, let me be very clear on the matter. The woman is evil incarnate. For you to question the existence of Satan or the existence of his minions is to question one's belief in God. Is that what you are implying? You must remember there are both good and evil, and evil takes many forms.'

'Of course not, Eminence. I am very sorry.'

'Good. To answer your question about the words she spoke in Aramaic, they are the same she has repeated multiple times over the years: *He who was cast out of Heaven and thrown into the lake of fire will pass his own Judgement one day.*' Sighing, he continued, 'Father Francis told you once that there are seven prophets to warn man of the coming judgement. You should know that his Holiness, Pope Nicholas, and I are not entirely convinced of that.'

He started to speak, but the cardinal held up his hand for silence.

'As I have said, Father Francis was a devout servant of the church. His visions were in service to the church. As I have already explained, the same cannot be said of Adelina. The other five, well, we do not know their purpose. Nor will we ever know. Not all gifts are good, Joseph, just as all gifts do not come from God. Father Francis also told you to have more faith in the power of evil, as well as that of good. You would do well to heed his advice.'

Deep brooding etched his thin face until he muttered hoarsely, 'I have only three more questions for you, Eminence. Why does she stay here? What prevents her from leaving? And am I still required to be her caretaker twice a day?'

'We have doubled the number of Swiss Guard outside of her door, but to be very clear, it is doubtful they could stop her should she decide to leave. I don't think she will, though. She stays here in the Vatican to torment us, to mock us with her presence. And yes, Father Joseph. It is imperative you continue your meetings with her. You have no alternative in the matter, my son.'

* * *

In the darkened hallway, four Swiss Guardsmen stood a silent watch outside the bedchamber of Sister Adelina, two on either side of the door. Joseph's knock was answered by the familiar rasping voice he had come to dread.

'Come in, Father Joseph.'

He entered the small room, carrying her dinner tray. Every step he took toward her bedside table, Illumined only by a single candle, increased his sense of foreboding. 'I have your dinner, Sister. How are you feeling this evening?'

She took her time before replying to him, deciding her words carefully. In a voice that rattled his core, she said, 'So, Father Joseph. I see I no longer hold the little secret of my identity over you.'

'How do you know that, Sister Adelina?'

'I know all your thoughts. I see everything you have ever seen and done. You hide no secrets from me. I know your mother was a bitch and a whore. Did you know that, false priest?'

'You lie, old woman," Joseph replied in a voice husky with fear.

Sister Adelina's dry chuckle made his skin prickle.

'Your mother laid down in bed with three lovers before your father. She spread her legs for men; their silver coins put bread on her table. She waits for you with open arms in the eternal fire. Yes, false priest, that is where you will spend eternity because I know your sins, too. I know you stole as a young man to feed your family and took your god's name in vain when your mother was on her deathbed. When you lay down to sleep at night, you touch yourself with visions of women you can never have. You have sinned many times, false priest. Judgement Day will soon be upon you and mankind. On the morning Christ was nailed to the wooden cross, the fate of all men was sealed. Your god's greatest lie of all was that there would one day be salvation. Hear my words. If ever there was a promise of salvation, it has long since been broken. Only those who are free of sin and asked for forgiveness of their sins at the very moment of their death will pass through the gates of Heaven. The number will be very small, old man. My master waits to reap the remainder of the unforgiven.'

EIGHTEEN

CAMINO DE SANTIAGO, SPAIN.

August 31, 2030.

A single star off to the north was the only speck of light against the black, velvety night sky. A breeze blowing through his window felt cool against his face as Eberhardt rested on his small cot, staring at the candle on his nightstand. The flickering flame's simplistic beauty held him spellbound for the moment. Two open books were propped up next to him: his Bible and a book from the monastery's library detailing the ravage of the Bubonic Plague. He turned his attention away from the candle and read from his Bible.

Then I saw in heaven another sign, great and awe-inspiring: seven angels with the seven last plagues, for through them God's fury is accomplished. Judgement Day was drawing near at hand.

It was as tangible as the wind through his window. His dreams detailed every moment in the most horrific detail. *Soon.*

The first angel went and poured out his bowl on the earth. Festering and ugly sores broke out on those who had the mark of the beast or worshiped its image. The second angel poured out his bowl on the sea. The sea turned to blood like that from a corpse; every creature in the sea died. The third angel poured out his bowl on the rivers and springs of water. These also turned to blood. The fourth angel poured out his bowl on the sun. It was given the power to burn people with fire. People were burned by the scorching heat and blasphemed the name of God who had the power over these plagues, but they did not repent or give him glory. The fifth angel poured out his bowl on the throne of the beast. Its kingdom was plunged into darkness, and people bit their tongues in pain and blasphemed the God of heaven because of their pains and sores. But they did not repent of their works. The sixth angel emptied his bowl on the great river Euphrates. Its water was dried up to prepare the way for the kings of the East. The seventh angel poured out his bowl into the air. A loud voice came out of the temple from the throne, saying, 'It is done.' Then there were lightning flashes, rumblings, and peals of thunder, and a great earthquake. It was such a violent earthquake that there has never been one like it since the human race began on earth.

Eberhardt smiled to himself. How foolish was man to believe in the promise of eternal salvation? God had poured out his wrath in judgement many times throughout history, and He was preparing to do it once more. The first had been on Adam in the Garden of Eden. Then, the great flood that destroyed the entire world save for Noah, his wife, and their family. Sodom and Gomorrah were demolished with both fire and brimstone. Now, judgement would come in the form of fire, water, famine, and plague. He had seen the fires spreading across the northern and western hemispheres. The ash and smoke blocked out all sunlight for many years, plunging the earth into darkness and causing a worldwide famine. Recent news was circulating in the monastery of the hurricanes and torrential rains flooding the Netherlands. *Water.* His dreams showed him of a plague originating in Europe and spreading like wildfire via every species of rat and bird.

The first angel went and poured out his bowl on the earth. Festering and ugly sores broke out on those who had the mark of the beast or worshiped its image.

No place on earth would be spared. Man, woman, and child would turn on each other until His judgement was complete.

Outside of his window, thunder began its rumbling, and a bolt of lightning flashed in the darkness.

NINETEEN

SAINT VERAN, FRANCE.

September 10, 2030.

Kneeling in the third pew, Clem finished her simple prayer, asking for God's love and protection over her parents and sister. Her mother and father had been married in this church, and she and her sister, Sophie, received the holy sacrament of baptism less than thirty steps from where she sat. Though she had attended mass there every Sunday since her birth, she felt like a stranger inside of God's house. She eyed the large crucifix hanging above the alter. The sight of Jesus nailed to the cross, blood dripping down his forehead from the crown of thorns and his side where the Roman spear had pierced him, frightened her more so at this moment. Father Nicholas Chabot had given many sermons from the altar before her, stating Jesus Christ's crucifixion had been for the redemption of all mankind. Clementina Voyant bowed her head again, wondering if it had all been a lie.

She heard the muffled voices of her mother and father talking with Father Nicholas behind the closed doors of his office. Her nightmares were getting worse, and her parents decided to seek guidance from the church. *As if the church, Father Nicholas, or anyone could help her.* The father's heavy wooden office door creaked opened and startled Clem from her thoughts. Straining to smile, her parents walked quietly toward her pew and sat down next to her.

Placing a hand under her daughter's small face, her mother lifted it gently. 'Father Nicholas would like to see you now, little Clem.'

Clem stood up slowly, giving her legs a moment to work through the pins and needles prickling her skin after kneeling for too long. Giving her mother and father a brave smile, she entered the small office.

'Please come in, Clementina, and sit down.' The father motioned to one of the two overstuffed chairs in front of his large desk.

Clem gave him a nervous grin. 'Thank you, Father.'

'As I am sure you are aware, your parents and I have been in discussion concerning unpleasant dreams you have been having of late.' Father Nicholas paused and eyed the young girl before him. Softening his voice, he said, 'Would you like to talk with me about what is troubling you, my child?'

She fidgeted in her seat, uncertain of where to begin.

'I know this must be difficult for you, my child, but I assure you ..."

Clem blurted out. 'You will be angry with me and tell my parents, and then they will be angry with me, too.'

Sitting on the corner of his desk near her, he reassured her the best he knew how. 'I will not be angry with you and neither will your parents. You have my word on that, little Clem. Please tell me of these dreams you have been having, my child.'

Unconvinced, she felt she had no choice in the matter. *Perhaps no one would be angry, especially Mother, because dreams cannot be controlled.* 'I have bad dreams every night about rats, Father. They are everywhere I look. They are large and black; they attack people and eat them. I have also had bad dreams where everything is on fire. The whole planet seems to be burning. Dead people are piled high in the streets, and no one bothers to bury them or to pray over them.'

Father Nicholas was aghast and rose from where he had been leaning against the desk to sit in his chair – a look of horror was etched across his face. 'Little Clem, you poor child. Why did you not discuss this with your parents sooner? You should not have suffered with this burden alone. Is there anything else you wish to tell me before I speak with your mother and father?'

She wanted to continue but hesitated. 'No, Father. There is nothing else. You are not angry with me, are you?'

'Of course not, dear child, and your parents will not be either. I can assure you of that. Please ask your mother and father to come back into my office. You can wait in the church for us.'

* * *

Once again kneeling in the pew of the third row, she bowed her head in prayer. This time, she prayed Father Nicholas had been truthful with her. Raising her eyes to the crucifix, she thought of the terrified look on Father Nicholas's face when she told him of her nightmares. It was for the best that she had not told him about her vision of standing on the hillside, looking down on the crucifixion of Christ ... or of His terrible words of retribution.

TWENTY

PARIS, FRANCE.

September 21, 2030.

They had been saving their money for over two years: Paris, France – a second honeymoon. She leaned her head against her husband's shoulder as they strolled hand-in-hand in the moonlight along the River Seine. It all felt magical. Tomorrow, they would tour the Eiffel Tower and the Louvre to see the Mona Lisa, followed by a late lunch at La Table du Marquis. Her husband turned to her and held her face close to his as they shared a kiss, softly at first and then with more passion. She felt her cheeks flush and her breath quicken.

Pulling back slightly, she gently put her fingertips to her husband's lips. 'Later,' she said to him with promise in her eyes.

Several yards below the two lovers, near the river's edge, lay the remains of a dead house cat killed and partially eaten by rats less than an hour before their arrival. The carcass was swarming with thousands of fleas in search of a warmer host. Unbeknownst to them, the young couple transported hundreds of tiny hitchhikers as they slowly made their way back to their hotel. Along the way, they infected four other couples enjoying the peacefulness of the evening and a young artist painting a landscape with the moon as his backdrop. Back at their hotel, they infected the doorman and a bellhop as well as three adults and two small children on the elevator. Their romantic night in the City of Lights would be their last.

When they woke the next morning, her husband complained of a migraine and a sore throat while she had cramps and felt feverish. They were both dead before breakfast was served.

The plague had begun in Europe.

TWENTY-ONE

CENTER FOR DISEASE CONTROL
HEADQUARTERS, ATLANTA, GEORGIA.

September 23, 2030. 10:10 A.M.

Embassy of the United States, Paris, France.
2 Avenue Gabriel, 75008.
September 22, 2030.

Dr. Marjorie Roberts
Director, CDC.

REF: The Special Consular Services Unit of the American Citizen Services Section: Death Notice.

Dr. Roberts:

On September 22, 2030, this office received notice that two American citizens, MR. JAMES NOLAN, and MRS. KATHERINE NOLAN, HUSBAND and WIFE, were transported to Saint-Louis Hospital, 1 Claude Vellefaux Avenue, Paris. Both parties were declared deceased at time of admittance. Please refer to death certificate and accompanying memo marked for your eyes only. REPEAT: FOR YOUR EYES ONLY.

Sincerely,
Mr. Gerald T. Spencer
Director, Special Consular Services Unit.

Dr. Roberts read the letter placed on her desk for the third time. Hands shaking, she picked up the attached memo and death certificates.

MEMO

Deaths of MR. and MRS. JAMES NOLAN were caused by a new variant of Yersinia pestis. REPEAT. NEW VARIANT. Numerous flea bites were discovered on both of the deceased. Conclusion is that Europe may be facing a new outbreak of Bubonic Plague. Mr. and Mrs. James Nolan arrived in Paris, France, on September 19, 2030. Time: 1615 hrs. Flight number: 201, Air France from Philadelphia International Airport. Deaths occurred within 3 days of arrival. Several additional deaths reported, including employees and other guests at the hotel Mr. and Mrs. James Nolan were registered at. Small outbreaks have been reported in the following countries: Italy, Germany, Russia, Spain. At this time, 47 deaths have been reported from countries listed. There have been no survivors. Tissue and blood samples are enclosed for your private analysis.

The small box sitting on her desk drew her attention. It was clearly marked *Biohazard. UN 2814.* Shipments of biohazard-labeled boxes were a daily occurrence at the Center for Disease Control, but this one was different. It had been hand-delivered by an armed courier and contained a substance she had feared all her adult life.

She lifted the small box with trembling hands and took it into her private lab adjoining her office. The laboratory's containment rooms ranged from the lowest bio-safety level (BSL-1) to the highest bio-safety level (BSL-4). The BSL-4 room consisted of multiple containment units, airflow systems, and maximum sealed containers that no biohazard known to man could escape from. She put the small package into one of the medium-sized containers and closed the lid; an audible hissing sound signified the seal was complete. Donning her positive-pressure personnel suit with respirator and protective gloves, Maggie sat down at her workstation and wondered how much time was left for the human race.

TWENTY-TWO

FEDERAL EMERGENCY MANAGEMENT
AGENCY, WASHINGTON, D.C.

September 23, 2030. 10:45 A.M.

Make the phone call. George's head was throbbing. *The matter is out of your hands. Make the damn phone call and be done with it.*

Moments ago, he had received a phone call from the president's secretary, Abigail Fitzgerald. President Holder wanted answers concerning the stability of Yellowstone National Park, and he wanted those answers now. Ms. Fitzgerald had relayed the president's order in her usual curt tone. He was to send in another team led by Dr. Stoner to Yellowstone National Park.

When he had inquired why the president had not phoned him directly, her response had been just as blunt. 'President Holder does not wish to speak with you directly at this time, Mr. Adams. Carry out your instructions.' She had hung up before he could reply any further.

He dialed the number.

* * *

He was not a man prone to anger, preferring to use his intelligence rather than his emotions when disagreements arose in the workplace or between friends; nevertheless, Mark was having a difficult time controlling his temper. 'Why me, George? You know what I went through at Yellowstone. I witnessed the horrible death of one of my best friends. I am very sorry, George. I will not go back into that park ever again.'

George let out a slow breath before he responded. 'This is not a request, Mark. It is an order issued by the president. To answer your question concerning why he picked you, well, I would think that would be more than obvious to a man with your considerable intellect.'

The words hung in the air for a brief, awkward moment. 'I beg your pardon? What the hell does that mean?'

'It means ... when you send a detailed report concerning the stability of the super volcano beneath Yellowstone to the president of the United States behind my back, ..."

Mark interrupted. 'I had no idea I was required to consult with *you* prior to corresponding with President Holder. I will resign from my position with U.S.G.S., effective immediately, if I am to be ordered back to Yellowstone National Park.'

George's anger was simmering. The conversation was going downhill quickly, and he needed to correct it. Not only because Mark was his colleague, but he was one of his oldest and dearest friends. He swallowed nervously. 'I'm sorry, Mark. I know how much Ben's death affected you. He was one of my best friends, too. I don't mean to put you on the spot, but the president knows you are the best man for this assignment. Besides that, your country needs you. If Yellowstone blows, you have some idea of how many deaths will take place. We need to have answers, and we can only get them from you.' He paused before adding, 'Please, Mark.'

Dr. Stoner felt drained of emotion as he sighed in despair. 'You make a persuasive argument. I'll leave immediately, but I'm not sure if Dr. Peterson will be accompanying me'

'Thank you. I will inform President Holder that you have agreed. As for Dr. Peterson, she is insignificant to your mission. We both know the only reason she was included the last time was at the request of Ben. Despite that, if you can persuade her to go with you, I think it might do her some good.'

'I will try. Perhaps it will do some good for both of us. Goodbye, my friend. I will be in touch with you the minute I have something to report.'

As George hung up his phone, he wondered if he had just sent one of his few remaining friends to his death.

TWENTY-THREE

THE WHITE HOUSE, WASHINGTON, D.C.

September 24, 2030. 9:00 A.M.

The White House aide stepped into the Oval Office corridor. The diminutive woman sitting in the waiting room was not more than five feet tall and appeared smaller than she was slouched over in her chair, smoking a cigarette, and studying the secure laptop perched on the coffee table in front of her. It was frowned upon for anyone to smoke in the White House, apart from the president's occasional pipe use. Before the aide could mutter a word, Dr. Roberts jumped to her feet and glared at him with the intense gaze of a predatory hawk.

The cigarette still dangling from the corner of her mouth, she asked, 'Is the president ready to see me now?'

He was caught off guard by the woman's abrupt manner and her demand versus a statement. He cleared his throat before answering. 'Yes, ma'am. President Holder will see you now. But I have to ask that you put out your cigarette before entering the Oval Office. Smoking is prohibited in the White House.'

'Young man, I know for certain that Henry smokes a pipe, and I don't put out a half-smoked cigarette for anyone. Now, lead the way or get out of the way."

President Holder stood and smiled warmly as Maggie entered his office. "I can always tell when you are anywhere in the White House. For a small woman, you have a loud voice.'

'Never mind that, Henry. I was kept cooling my heels long enough in that shoebox you call a waiting room. I told you on the phone to have O'Henry and some of your military men here with you. Where the hell are they?'

The president's aide, for his part, stood in the doorway with his mouth agape. He had never witnessed such disrespect toward the president.

"Jim, would you ask National Security Advisor O'Henry and Admiral Stockton to join us, please?'

'Of course, Mr. President.'

He could sense his longtime friend was in no joking mood and seemed terrified. 'Maggie,' he said, 'please take a seat and tell me what this is all about.'

Before she could respond, there was a knock at the door. Both O'Henry and the admiral entered the Oval Office and took their seats on the sofa. Maggie paced furiously across the thick carpet as the three men watched her chain smoke. The president placed his hands tenderly on her shoulders, trying to calm her and guide her to her seat. 'Maggie, please sit down and tell us what this is all about.'

She looked up slowly into his eyes, and momentarily, he saw a blankness as if she did not recognize him, but the fear was still visible on her tiny face. She sat, tapped a fresh cigarette from her pack, and lit it.

'Henry ...' she started to say but was hesitant on where to begin.

The president took her hand in his and felt it trembling. 'What is it, Maggie?'

She finally looked at the three men seated around her. Without a second thought, she opened her laptop and punched in the security code.

***

'Are you sure it is a new variant?' O'Henry leaned forward in his seat, waiting for her response. There was a note of skepticism in his deep voice.

Maggie glared at him, but before she could respond to his question, President Holder interjected. 'William, Dr. Roberts is the leading bacteriologist and microbiologist in the world. If she states this is a new variant, then it is.'

O'Henry arched his eyebrows. 'Of course, Mr. President. At the moment, I do not see any cause for alarm. According to Dr. Robert's report from our embassy in France, dated September 23rd, there have only been 47 deaths reported so far within the boundaries of five countries. I, of course, do not wish to minimize those 47 unfortunate deaths, but it is hardly cause for ...'

'You don't wish to *minimize*? You pompous jackass! How dare you?'

The president stood up and held out his hands to settle things down. 'Please, Maggie.'

Before he could utter another word, she lowered her gaze back to her computer screen, which flashed with an ominous reddish glow. The men watched as her facial features went from anger to disbelief and then horror. Maggie shook her head. 'This is unimaginable.' Dr. Roberts felt a rising dread as she continued to stare at her computer screen.

President Holder sat down next to her and stared at the laptop as it continued to emit that strange reddish glow. 'What is it, Maggie?'

Maggie raised her eyes to look at the president, who was transfixed on her computer.

'Henry,' she whispered, 'it's spreading faster than even I thought it could have. Seven more European countries have reported outbreaks in the past twenty-four hours. The death toll stands at over 8,000.'

'My God,' Admiral Stockton said in a voice hoarse with raw emotion. 'From 47 deaths to over 8,000 in 24 hours?'

President Holder stood up slowly, returned to his desk, and sat down. The air inside the Oval Office seemed stiflingly hot and stagnant, and his head was throbbing. He returned his focus to his longtime friend. 'Maggie, what can we do to help? We must have a response to this crisis.'

She seemed to not hear his words at first, so he repeated himself. She gazed at him with a sadness in her eyes he knew he would never be able to forget. 'I don't know, Henry,' she replied huskily. 'When I received the specimen yesterday from France, I took it into my personal biosecurity facility to conduct my own tests.' She shook her head and mumbled. 'It was unlike anything I have ever seen before. The cell culture changed with every test I conducted. The way it mutated seemed almost *evil*. It was as if it ..."

O'Henry interrupted her as he rubbed his hand thoughtfully over his beard. 'Dr. Roberts, it seems highly unlikely a bacteria strain could change at such a pace. I think you are being overly emotional with your statement of it being evil.'

Her eyes narrowed as she stood to her full height of four feet eleven inches and turned her gaze toward the national security advisor. 'I would appreciate intelligent comments, *if you have any*, Mr. O'Henry. With that said, I seriously doubt you have more knowledge in my field than I do. There is very little that is impossible in nature. You would do well to keep that in mind, sir.' She began to pace the Oval Office once more. 'I have asked my most trusted colleagues to conduct their own tests, which they are continuing with as we speak. There have been no success rates to report. Nothing we have tried has worked to stop the growth of the specimen. I have isolated the cause to be the Xenopsylia cheopis, or Oriental Rat Flea, an important vector of the plague; it is the Pneumonic version of the disease, the most difficult to treat. It is the only form of the disease that can be spread from person to person in a variety of ways, such as through the air in droplets when one sneezes or coughs, or by touching any surface, like a doorknob or phone that was recently handled by a sick individual.'

'Maggie, you mentioned that the *vector*, as you referred to it, was the Oriental Rat Flea. As I know you are aware, China has seen a recent outbreak in the Inner Mongolia region, which has resulted in the deaths of over 522 of its citizens. Could it be possible that the outbreak in China and Europe are related?'

'It is very possible, Henry. At this point, nothing is off the table. I have been in touch with a colleague in China who is an epidemiologist. He tried to use the antibiotic Streptomycin, which in the past, was the most effective treatment against Yersinia pestis, but it proved to be useless. There have been no survivors in China. He reports some of the symptoms he has witnessed include sudden fever and chills, severe headache, and extreme weakness. He has also seen portions of the skin turn black and die, which is a symptom of Septicemic plague. I received an update on the status of China early this morning. The current death toll stands at 717 dead, but that is a rough estimation. Regardless, the outbreak in Europe is much worse. And it is spreading faster.'

Admiral Stockton shifted nervously before asking his question. 'Have there been any cases reported in the United States?'

'No, Admiral. Not that I am aware of." She paused and swallowed nervously. 'We need to take steps immediately to make every effort to prevent this outbreak, this *plague*, from reaching our shores and pray that it is not too late already.'

Unsettled, the president asked, 'What do you suggest, Maggie?'

She stared hard at the men and rested her focus on the president. 'You need to seal our borders, Henry. You need to do it now. No ships must be allowed to dock at any port of the United States. No plane must be allowed to land on U.S. soil. I repeat, you must do it before it is ...'

O'Henry's voice was sharp. 'Are you insane? You want us to close our borders based on a few thousand deaths that have occurred in Europe and Asia? Mr. President, I hope you are not going to consider this.'

The president anticipated a response from the scientist, but she sat with her head bowed low, silently brooding. 'Maggie,' he ventured, 'I need you to focus. There must be other alternatives you can provide me with. Shutting down all external transportation cannot be our only option.'

Hands clasped tightly on her lap, she slowly shook her head back and forth and murmured, 'Our time is limited.'

'Maggie, look at me. I need answers from you.' The president hesitated and drew in a deep breath, unsure of how hard he should press her. 'I need those answers right now.'

'My God,' she whispered under her breath and looked at the man staring back at her. There was an odd, puzzled expression on her small face. 'I have given you my only option. No, let me clarify that. I have given you *your* only option. I have no cure.' Her voice rose, and she seemed to be on the verge of hysteria. 'Do you understand that, Henry? There is *no* cure, and we may never have one. The damn bacteria culture changed multiple times within minutes right in front of me. If you let this plague reach our shores, you will bear witness to the deaths of millions of Americans.' She paused to let her words sink in. 'That is, of course, if it has not already.'

Admiral Stockton groaned and shook his head. 'At any given moment, there are hundreds of flights in the air bound for the United States. How do we go about turning them back? Even if we were able to turn those flights around, which is doubtful, where would they go? They will be running low on fuel, unable to return to Europe or Asia. We must allow them to land, and at the very least, refuel.'

O'Henry felt a sudden rush of anger. 'I cannot believe what I am hearing. You actually want to shut our borders down?' He glanced around the Oval Office, focusing on no one in particular. 'And what do we do if the planes will not turn around or abide by our orders? We must be compassionate, Mr. President!' He turned on Maggie. 'What do we do, Dr. Roberts? What do you suggest we do?'

Maggie took in a deep breath and exhaled slowly. 'Mr. O'Henry, if there are any cases of this plague on board any of those flights coming into the United States, then those people are already dead. There may be some who are immune to this disease, but there has been no evidence to support that assertion. So, to answer your question, if the pilot of any plane or the captain of any ship will not heed our order ...,' she paused, 'then they must be destroyed.'

The men were stunned into silence by what they had just heard. President Holder was the first to regain his composure.

'You can't mean that, Maggie. What about a quarantine period? What about refueling the planes and giving them a chance to return to their location of origin?'

'You haven't been listening to me, Henry. There is no cure for this bacteria. As I have already stated, if one person is infected on board either plane or ship, then we must assume they are all infected, and hence, will all eventually die. As far as a quarantine, well, quarantines have been breached in the past. The same goes for your refueling option. We must not take any chances. Henry, when the plague, or *Black Death*, as some like to refer to it, swept across Europe during the fourteenth century, the estimates ranged from 75 to 200 million dead. I must repeat myself. I have *no way* to combat this disease, and I may not have a way to combat this disease in the future. You must act before it is too late.'

The president sat in shock, feeling the weight of the world on his shoulders. Looking at Admiral Stockton, he said. 'James, get General Burton at Central Command and General Wilson at the Pentagon on the phone. I need to speak with both men immediately.'

O'Henry came off the sofa in a rush. 'Mr. President, you cannot ...'

He held up his hand to silence him. 'I do not believe I have any choice in the matter, William. May God have mercy on me for what I am about to do.'

Admiral Stockton went to the sideboard and picked up the secure phone. 'Mr. President, would you like me to tell them?'

Patting his friend on the back, the president said, 'Thank you for the kind offer, James, but it is a phone call I have to make, myself.'

TWENTY-FOUR

ATLANTIC OCEAN, EAST COAST OF THE UNITED STATES OF AMERICA.

September 24, 2030. 11:47 A.M.

The Marine pilot was stationed in Norfolk, Virginia. All hell had just broken loose less than fifteen minutes ago due to the emergency briefing of his squadron. This had immediately been followed by the order to scramble their F-35B Lightning II Stealth fighter jets. At the moment, he was passing over the Chesapeake Bay Bridge Tunnel. The cargo ships far below him were the problem of the U.S. Navy and Coast Guard. He and his fellow Marine and Navy pilots were responsible for the incoming commercial flights approaching the east coast of the United States. His orders were simple – order the planes to land at one of seven Air Force bases the president authorized for refueling only: Andrews AFB, Maryland; Charleston AFB, South Carolina; Hickam AFB, Hawaii; Lackland AFB, Texas; Macdill AFB, Florida; McChord AFB, Washington State, and Travis AFB, California. The commercial pilots were to be informed during refueling that no one was allowed to exit the plane. Once refueling was complete, the aircraft was to return to its country of origin. If there was failure to comply with the order, the aircraft would be destroyed. Any attempt to land anywhere other than the bases authorized would result in the destruction of the aircraft. More ominous than that had been the order if the commercial pilots mentioned any illness or medical emergency on board their flights, then the planes were to be shot down over the ocean without warning. These orders had been issued by the president of the United States and relayed by Major General Bill Tyler, in person.

There had been a brief uproar at rollcall, and several senior officers objected immediately, but the general provided a brief explanation. 'A potentially incurable disease, a form of the Bubonic Plague, has struck Europe and Asia. If it makes its way onto American soil, millions will die. Follow your orders or face immediate court martial. End of discussion.'

The pilots boarded their fighter jets and hit the afterburners.

* * *

His F-35B Lightning II Stealth Fighter was equipped with a GAU-22/A four-barrel Gatling gun with a rate of fire of 3,000 shots per minute. In addition, there were twin sets of AIM-9x Sidewinder missiles mounted under each wing. He was tracking eleven inbound commercial flights on his radar screen. His single fighter could have easily handled all eleven, but that was unnecessary. He had more than enough company in the skies around him covering the entire perimeter of the United States. The commercial flights had received their reroute instructions from various control towers where they were initially scheduled to land. He had to ensure the civilian pilots followed those instructions to the letter. He checked his radar again. Nine of the eleven flights reported the instructions were received and recalculated their course to Andrews Air Force Base in Maryland. Each of the redirected flights had a military escort riding its tail to make sure the course was maintained. Regarding the remaining two flights, an Airbus A380 heading for Newark Airport in New Jersey and a Boeing 767 bound for Ronald Reagan National Airport in Virginia, he radioed his wingman to contact and escort the Virginia-bound flight. He would take up a position with the Airbus.

* * *

He maneuvered his fighter jet to within 300 yards of the massive aircraft and established radio contact. From this distance, he had a visual on the cockpit. Something was wrong. Where there should have been three people at the very least on a long flight coming in from Europe – the pilot, co-pilot, and the flight engineer/navigator – there was only one man visible.

'Bravo 1 9er to Flight 313. You have received your instructions to redirect to Andrews AFB, Maryland. Acknowledge, over.'

'Bravo 1 9er, this is the co-pilot, Flight 313. We have a medical emergency on board, and we need to land ASAP at Newark International. My pilot is unconscious. Numerous passengers are also ill. Request you give us clearance and escort us to Newark Airport, over.'

The Marine captain touched the crucifix that hung around his neck. *Damn it.* His orders were any mention of illness required an immediate destruction of the aircraft. He tried again. 'Negative, Flight 313. Change course and comply with your instructions. You are not cleared for Newark, over.'

'What the hell is going on? I have over 840 passengers on board. Women and children are sick. We must land at Newark. It's the closest airport that can accommodate us, over.'

He rubbed his crucifix once more. It had been a gift to him from his mother on the day he became an altar boy at the age of nine. He had worn it ever since and taken a ribbing from his fellow Marines for wearing it. The fire controls for the AIM-9x Sidewinder missiles were near his right hand. He flipped the two switches, arming all four. One would have been more than enough, but he wanted no chance of any suffering. There was a momentary jolt to his jet as the missiles left his undercarriage followed by a massive fireball three seconds later.

He disengaged from his parachute. He had just killed over 800 men, women, and children. No. He had *murdered* them all in cold blood. He asked for God's forgiveness, clutched his crucifix tightly in his left hand, and pulled the ejection lever.

TWENTY-FIVE

WHITE HOUSE BRIEFING ROOM, WASHINGTON, D.C.

September 24, 2030. 1:30 P.M.

There was an unusual hushed silence as President Holder approached the podium and quietly surveyed the large group of reporters seated in front of him. He was not only addressing the American people but giving an emergency presidential address to the entire world. Every major news source in the Washington, D.C. area was in attendance. In addition, multiple foreign syndicates had their cameras trained on his every move. Every word spoken would be broadcast live across the entire planet. At his side were Vice President Timmons, National Security Advisor O'Henry, and CDC Director Roberts. Admiral Stockton stood off to one side of the podium in the event any questions concerning the military arose. The president reviewed his prepared notes. His hands were shaking, and he was perspiring heavily. He looked at his press secretary, Rose Tyler. She gave him a nervous smile as he looked back into the dozens of cameras trained on him.

Standing tall, the president spoke in a clear and solemn voice as he addressed the nation and the world. 'Ladies and gentlemen,' he began, 'on the 23rd of September, the Center for Disease

Control in Atlanta, Georgia, received a communication from the American Embassy in France concerning the deaths of two American citizens. It has been confirmed that the cause of those two deaths was due to a new variant of the Bubonic Plague.' He paused to take a sip of water before redirecting his focus back on the cameras. 'As of this morning, we have had reports of over 8,000 deaths across Europe and over 700 in China.'

There were numerous gasps of alarm that came from the reporters in attendance; several sprang to their feet and left the room, undoubtedly to phone their loved ones in Europe. He held out his hands to settle everyone down. 'Please. We need to remain calm and behave in an orderly manner.'

Several reporters stood to ask questions, but the press secretary took charge. 'Please return to your seats and hold all your questions until the end of the president's briefing.'

There was an awkward silence while the TV cameras rolled on the president who appeared uncharacteristically uncertain about the situation. But he straightened his tie and continued. 'Currently, we do not have a cure for this new variant, and that is why I have taken the unprecedented step of securing our borders. No planes or ships originating outside of the continental United States will be allowed to enter United States soil.'

Once more, there was a flurry of commotion, and every reporter had his or her hand in the air. Rose again tried to restore order, but President Holder motioned her back to her seat. He turned and faced the horde of reporters. 'If everyone would please return to their seats, I will answer all your questions.' He scanned the press corps, looking for the toughest investigative reporter. 'Let's start with you, Ryan.'

The reporter got to his feet quickly. 'Mr. President, there have been unconfirmed reports about a civilian airliner being shot down off the east coast by our military. Is there any truth to that report?'

He stared hard at the reporter; Ryan never disappointed in going right for his throat. 'I am sorry to say it is true. The Marine pilot was following ...'

There were multiple angry outbursts from the press and others in attendance. Several Secret Service agents and two Marines in full dress blue uniforms moved forward to stand in front of the podium, but the president motioned for them to step back. 'I understand how disturbing and upsetting this news is, but I will have order. To continue with my answer, the Marine pilot was acting on my directive. Every flight attempting to land in the United States was ordered to divert to specific Air Force bases around the country for refueling purposes only and return to its country of origin. The airliner in question disobeyed those instructions and reported numerous passengers were afflicted with an illness on board. I felt there was no ...'

'So, you ordered an unarmed civilian flight to be shot down?'

He lowered his head, wiped his eyes, and looked at the reporter who had interrupted him. In a voice barely above a whisper, he said, 'Yes. I ordered it to be shot down. I do not believe I had any choice. If the plague reaches our shores,' he paused, 'I have been advised that millions may die as a result."

A reporter took to his feet slowly. There were tears streaming down his face, and he made no attempt to wipe them away. 'And who advised you of that, Mr. President? Who was it that advised you to murder American citizens, you bastard?'

Maggie Roberts moved to the podium and stood in front of her longtime friend. 'I advised President Holder to take these drastic actions.'

The reporter glared at Maggie Roberts with hatred in his eyes. 'Who the hell are you?'

'My name is Dr. Roberts, and I am the director of the CDC based in Atlanta. My colleagues and I have been studying these bacteria nonstop since we received samples yesterday. It changes form at will and has resisted every antibiotic we have subjected it to. There is no current cure for this disease. Nor do I foresee a cure anytime soon ... if ever.' She swallowed down the lump in her throat and said, 'President Holder is unaware, but moments ago, I received an update from Europe and Asia. The death toll has climbed to over 90,000 from just 8,000 this morning. The world has been infected with a new form of the Black Death. People are literally dying in the streets of Europe as we speak.'

TWENTY-SIX

YELLOWSTONE NATIONAL PARK, WYOMING.

September 25, 2030.

He pushed his plate away from him; his appetite was nonexistent.

'Something wrong with them ham and eggs, boy?' Jambe asked while entering the mess hall from the kitchen, wiping his hands on his overalls.

'No. Nothing's wrong. Just not in the mood for breakfast this morning.'

Jambe poured himself a cup of black coffee and sat down on the bench across from Ethan. 'Listen here. I know that lady scientist coming back to the park has your stomach all in knots but not eating won't help matters any. Besides that, you know my number one mess hall rule is that you clean your plate. Didn't your mother teach you that when you was growing up?' Jambe slid the plate back across the wooden table. 'Finish your breakfast before I do something to hurt you, boy.'

'You're like an old mother hen, Jambe, but you're right. Going hungry won't solve my problems.' Ethan picked up his fork and broke one of the egg yolks. 'Not too bad, but I prefer them cooked a little longer.'

He gave Ethan a rare smile. 'Cook 'em, yourself, next time. You know my number two rule is no complaining about the food.'

Raindrops slid down the glass of the window across from the roaring fireplace. The wind was beginning to pick up.

'You and me, Ethan ... we're friends, right?'

'Sure. You remind me of my grandfather in some ways.'

'What ways you talking 'bout, boy?'

'Well, you're gruff like he was when he tried to hide his feelings; you speak your mind in the same way, too. Small things like that.'

Jambe sniffed and wiped his nose on his sleeve. 'Mind if I ask a personal question?'

'Not at all; we're friends just like you said.'

'You in love with that young woman?'

Temporarily stung by the question, Ethan's shoulders drooped before he responded. 'Is it that obvious?'

'You been moping around camp ever since she left back in June.' Jambe hesitated. 'At first, I thought it might have had something to do with that fella's death. Now, I'm not sure. How does she feel about you, boy?'

'I haven't heard from her since she left the park almost four months ago. That tells me everything I need to know. Besides, I'm too young for her.'

Jambe snorted. 'Hell, boy. You sure is dumb. Age ain't got nothing to do with love. Do I have to teach you everything about life?'

Before he could respond, the phone rang.

'Mess hall. Jambe speaking.'

Jambe, this is Lt. Spanyer. Is Ethan there?'

'He's sitting right here, Lieutenant, eating breakfast.'

'Tell him to finish up and report to headquarters. Dr. Stoner has arrived.'

* * *

Standing outside of the mess hall's front door, Ethan noticed the rain had abated but thick, blackened clouds still hung low in the sky. Down the dirt path near headquarters, a government limousine was driving away. *She is here. Now what?* He stepped

142

onto the muddy path with both of his hands thrust deep into his pockets. *Time to figure it out.*

* * *

Lt. Spanyer was waiting for him by the side entrance of the headquarters building when he walked up.

Ethan smiled. 'Good morning, Lieutenant. How are you today?'

'Never mind that, Ethan. I wanted to let you know before you go inside that I won't be making the trip with you.' He shrugged in annoyance. 'Dr. Stoner, for reasons known only to him, has requested I not accompany him into the field. Apparently, I make him uncomfortable.'

Ethan was confused. 'And Chief Miller is fine with it?'

'Chief Miller is not calling the shots right now, Ethan. Dr. Stoner is. He is here by orders of the president. Something big is in the air, and the chief is on edge. You're a good kid. If I were you, I would keep my head down low and do exactly as told. I wish I were going with you, but I'm not. Let's go inside. The chief is waiting.'

Chief Miller was seated at his desk. Dr. Stoner and another elderly gentleman were huddled on either side of him; all three were studying a large map of Yellowstone National Park spread out across the desk. Stacey was deep in thought, staring out the window of the office.

'You're late, Ranger Hardy. Take a seat.'

Ethan sat down nervously. The mood in the large room was uncomfortable. 'I'm sorry I'm late, sir. It will not happen again.'

Chief Miller leaned back in his chair. 'See that it doesn't. You, of course, know Dr. Stoner and Dr. Peterson.' Gesturing to the other man, he said, 'This is Dr. Albert King, a colleague of theirs.'

Dr. King looked up, nodded, and went back to studying the map in front of him.

'He will be accompanying you into the field.' Chief Miller glanced briefly at Dr. Stoner and then at Lt. Spanyer. 'As you may or may not be aware, the lieutenant will not be making this trip with you. There are two rookie rangers waiting outside with two

143

Smith

fully-equipped trucks. You will be in charge of those two rangers, Hardy, but you will take your orders from Dr. Stoner. Your orders from me are the same as last time: escort Dr. Stoner's party to any location within the park's boundaries. Are there any questions?'

Ethan snuck a brief glance at Stacey, who had still not turned around. 'No, sir. No questions.'

Chief Miller grunted his approval. 'Fine.'

A steady rain was falling as they exited headquarters. Drs. Stoner and King took their seats in the rear of the lead truck.

As Stacey was making her way toward the same truck, Ethan tapped her gently on the shoulder. 'Are you at least going to acknowledge me?'

Stacey turned around slowly. 'I'm sorry, Ethan. I want you to know I am very happy to see you again. I've missed you, but I'm extremely depressed about being back in Yellowstone so soon after Ben's death. Please understand my feelings. I just need a little space.'

Ethan was silent and thought she felt his disapproval. Smiling warmly at her, he said, 'I understand, Stacey. Will you ride in my truck, so we can talk?'

Stacey hesitated before touching his cheek with her fingertips. 'I'm sorry, Ethan. I think it would be best if I rode in the other truck with Mark.'

* * *

Ethan pulled his hat down lower to shield his face from the rain as he climbed into the front passenger seat of the rear truck. Johnny Taylor, the ranger seated behind the steering wheel, had only been in uniform for two weeks, and Ethan oversaw his training at the main gate. They exchanged nods of acknowledgement.

'Pull around to the side of their truck, so I can speak to Dr. Stoner. Then, we'll take the lead.'

Pulling alongside the other vehicle, Taylor turned to face Ethan. 'Hey, man. You feeling okay? You look kinda pissed off.'

'I'm fine, Johnny. Never did like being out in the rain.' Ethan got out and walked over to Mark's window. 'Good morning, Dr. Stoner. I am sorry we didn't get a chance to say hello back at headquarters.'

144

'Ah, young Ethan. No, we didn't have much time for pleasantries ... both Dr. King and I felt most unwelcomed by your chief. How are you, my boy?'

'I'm well, sir. Thank you. I didn't hear from Chief Miller what our destination would be this morning.'

'Silly me. Our first stop needs to be Mallard Lake Dome, followed by a trip to Grand Prismatic Springs in a few days' time. Are you familiar with those two regions?'

'I have been to both of those areas several times, sir. We should reach Mallard Lake by the early afternoon ...' Hardy tipped his head back slightly to look at the sky. 'Providing the weather cooperates with us, that is.'

'Let us be on our way, then, Ethan. We can't let the weather dictate our decisions, can we?'

Ethan looked over to where Stacey sat in the front seat. Her deadpan eyes were focused solely on the road ahead of her. Looking back at Mark, the elderly man had a thin smile but a worried expression on his face. 'No, sir. We can't let the weather stand in our way.'

Returning to his seat, he fell into a brooding silence. The long ride to Mallard Lake Dome was slow-going, especially when the rain turned into a torrential downpour – making their travel somewhat treacherous on the dirt roads. It was late evening when they arrived at their base camp.

Ethan stepped directly into a giant puddle as he climbed down from his truck, and muddy water filled his boot. 'Great. What else can go wrong?' he muttered to himself.

Taylor could not help but laugh. 'Nice going, Ethan.'

'Very funny. Let's find some high ground and get the tents set up.'

The ranger from the other truck joined them. Ethan had never met him before and held out his hand in greeting. 'I'm Ethan Hardy. What do I call you?'

'My name is Scott Taylor, sir. Most folks call me Casper, though, because of my hair.' With that, he pushed back his ranger hat, revealing a crewcut of solid white hair.

Ethan chuckled. He didn't look a day over eighteen years old. 'Sure. Casper it is, then. Do you and Johnny know each other?'

'Yes, sir. Johnny and I bunk together.'

'Listen, Casper,' Ethan said with a touch of exasperation in his voice. 'I only have a few month's seniority on both of you. Let's knock off the *sir* stuff. We'll just be friends and work side-by-side. Does that sound good to you?'

'Sounds great. Where do we start?'

'As I was telling Johnny, we need to find a relatively dry, high-ground area and set up the tents. You two can handle that job while I work on a firepit. The rain seems to be in a lull for the moment, so work fast.'

The sun was setting when Ethan finished. He added some small sticks and brush before hitting his flint against a flat rock to start the blaze – the way his father had taught him. Once the fire roared to life, he stood back and observed three tents had been erected around their campfire, and their trucks repositioned several yards away. *Perfect.* A reddish hue had taken over the twilight sky, and he smiled to himself ... no more rain tonight.

Casper approached him. 'Ethan, when do we eat? I'm hungry.'

'We eat when one of you cooks the franks and beans, my friend. Which one of you will it be? Mind you. Whoever doesn't cook has to clean up.'

Casper quickly set to making dinner, leaving his counterpart somewhat miffed.

Ethan clapped Johnny on the back in a friendly manner. 'You can do the cooking tomorrow night. Help me get some folding chairs out of the camper and set them around the fire.'

Stacey left her tent and walked over to join them. 'Is there anything I can do to help?'

A broad grin filled Ethan's face at the sound of her voice. 'We've got it but appreciate your offer. Have you seen Dr. Stoner and Dr. King?'

He noticed her returned smile did not reflect any emotion in her eyes. 'They are in their tent discussing tomorrow's plans. Would you like me to tell them dinner is ready?'

Ethan nodded. 'Yes, please.'

The wind was growing colder as they gathered around the fire and ate their dinner. The doctors kept to themselves with their heads bent low in quiet discussion, Casper and Johnny were debating the football season, and Ethan sat as close to Stacey as he dared.

Dr. Stoner stood, arched his back, and yawned. 'I believe I shall attempt to get some sleep. Are you coming, Dr. King? We have a busy day planned for tomorrow.'

Dr. King tapped his pipe on a nearby rock to clean it. 'I believe I will. The night air is most refreshing, but it tends to tire me out long before my accustomed bedtime. Goodnight, all.'

With that, both men disappeared into their tent. Johnny busied himself with cleaning up the plates while Casper got to his feet and walked into the nearby woods. Stacey watched him until he disappeared amongst the trees. She gave Ethan a quizzical look, and he winked at her.

'Nature's calling.'

She blushed in the firelight. 'I better answer the same call before I turn in for the night. Do you have any suggestions on where I should go?'

Ethan rose to his feet and pointed. 'There is a steep drop-off several hundred feet to your left – that would be a bad idea. Casper is over there behind the tents, so steer clear of his spot, and ..."

Stacey was hopping from one foot to the other. 'Come on, wise guy.'

Ethan smirked. 'I think you will be safe behind us. Watch out for rattlesnakes.'

When she returned, the fire had died down to embers, and Ethan was sitting alone. She sat down beside him and took his hand. 'I'm glad we are alone, Ethan. I think we should talk.'

'I'd like that a lot.'

'I never meant to hurt you, and I know I have been distant since I arrived. I hope ...'

He interrupted her. There was a note of pain in his voice mixed with a touch of anger. 'Were you ever planning to contact me again? I haven't heard from you since June, and I have left several voicemails at your office.'

'I know you have. And yes, I planned to talk with you when the time was right.' She put her hands over her eyes. 'When Ben died in that horrible way, I couldn't think straight. The nightmares – I ... I can still see the look of agony on his face. I never told you, but before we ended our relationship, Ben and I were talking about marriage.' She started to cry softly.

Ethan moved closer and put his arm around her shoulder. 'I'm so sorry, Stacey. I had no idea.'

They sat quietly for several minutes, holding each other tightly. Regaining her composure, she reached out her hands and cupped his face gently. In the stillness, they shared their first kiss.

'It's time for me to go to bed, Ethan Hardy. Please be patient with me.' She kissed him goodnight and stood up to go, but he reached for her hand.

'Stacey, before you go to your tent, have you ever heard the word *varlebena* before?'

'No. What does it mean?'

'It's an Apache word ... it means *forever*. That's how I feel about you. I just wanted you to know that.'

She kissed him one last time. 'Goodnight, Ranger Hardy.'

'Goodnight, Stacey.'

High overhead, an eagle took flight into the blackness of the night. It was heading eastward.

* * *

Ethan climbed into his sleeping bag and closed his eyes. The memory of tonight would last a lifetime, of that, he was certain. He rolled over, unzipped the tent flap, and peered out. The bright yellow full moon was casting its soft glow over the surrounding woods. Not for the first time, he considered what primitive men must have thought when they gazed upon it. He was uncertain if sleep would elude him or if it would be filled with dreams of her embrace and kisses. *Wait.* He did not seem to be dreaming anymore: no visions, no nightmares – at least none since Dr. Williams was killed. *Was there a connection?* Some sixth sense told him there was. He closed the tent flap against the bitter wind and fell fast asleep.

* * *

Mark bolted upright in his tent. He glanced at his watch; the luminous hands showed the time: 07:37. It should have been light outside, but it wasn't. Something was wrong, and at first, he had no idea what woke him until he felt it again. A chill raced down his spine; an ever-so-slight tremor stopped and restarted. It was stronger, steadier, and lasted approximately two minutes. He threw back the flap of his tent and raced outside. The horizon was an ugly shade of purple, and he could barely make out the sun behind the inky black clouds.

Ethan stepped out of his tent, yawning and rubbing the sleep from his eyes. 'What is it, Dr. Stoner? I felt the ground shake for a moment.'

Mark turned toward his young friend, fear clearly visible on his face. 'Wake Stacey, Ethan. Wake everyone, and *hurry*. I think we are in serious trouble.'

Ethan walked quickly toward Stacey's tent, but she was already dressed and exiting it.

She gave Ethan a quick nod and went to Mark's side. 'I felt it. Several times.'

The sound of wings beating the air caused all three to look skyward. Birds of every species were blackening the skies: swans, geese, ospreys, and eagles were flying as one and heading in the same direction, east.

Ethan turned to face Stacey with a puzzled expression on his face. 'What do you make of that? I have never seen birds act that way before.'

Before Stacey could reply, a grayish ash began falling, silently like dark snowflakes. Within moments, none of them could see their boots.

Mark grabbed Stacey by the shoulders. 'We need to go, *now*! Leave everything behind and get to the trucks.'

Dr. King, Casper, and Johnny jumped into one truck; Ethan, Stacey, and Dr. Stoner raced to the other truck.

Mark yelled at Ethan, 'There isn't a moment to lose. Get us to the main road immediately. *Let's go!*'

As Ethan gunned the truck's engine to life, a new massive tremor caused several nearby trees to fall, and a huge boulder rolled past their campsite. Momentarily, there was dead silence.

Deep underground, Yellowstone's Caldera was awaking after 700,000 years. Most scientists believed that the Caldera measured somewhere around 34 by 45 miles. *They were dead wrong.* In truth, Yellowstone's Caldera measured over 78 by 125 miles. It was believed that an unnamed chamber contained 11,200 cubic miles of magma, which when added to an already known chamber containing 2,500 miles of magma, could fill the Grand Canyon an estimated fourteen times. Previous estimates were highly inaccurate. Astonishingly, the massive magma reservoir could have filled the entire Grand Canyon well over 80 times, and at that very moment, all of it was making its way toward the surface.

If the team could have witnessed their seismometers in their tents, the devices were registering an earthquake magnitude of 11.9. The rupture in the earth created a fault length over 670 miles and was heading toward California's San Andreas Fault.

In a moment of finality, Ethan grabbed Stacey's hand tightly in his own as the ground beneath both trucks collapsed into an ocean of fire.

TWENTY-SEVEN

WHITE HOUSE BRIEFING ROOM, WASHINGTON D.C.

September 26, 2030. 1:10 P.M.

Three long tables lined with microphones, laptops, paper, and pens were joined end-to-end in front of the podium that bore the presidential seal. The press had not been invited to this briefing. In fact, they were not even aware the meeting was taking place. Every member of the media, including hundreds of reporters, were being kept behind barricades on the West Lawn. They had been denied access to the White House by presidential order.

President Holder sat at the center table with Vice President Timmons, National Security Advisor O'Henry, and Marine Corps General Tim Sterling. To the president's right sat Admiral Stockton, CDC Director Roberts, and FEMA Administrator Adams while Ms. Fitzgerald sat glassy-eyed with a tear-streaked face behind them.

Every scientist, mathematician, and physicist the White House could lay their hands on with such short notice were in the press section. Emergency lights flickered throughout the room – electricity only possible via several portable generators in the hallway. Though the meeting was yet to be called to order, there was a low murmur of nervous conversations filling the air.

Every eye turned his way when the president stood. He motioned for Abby to join him in the rear corner of the briefing room. 'Abby, I need you to hold it together for me.' His eyes pleaded with her to listen to him. 'Has there been any further word on my wife and son?'

She wiped her eyes and looked up at her friend and president. 'The news is the same, Henry. The Secret Service was able to get them on board their private jet, and they safely lifted off from Dallas Airport; however, there has been no contact since then.' She wiped her eyes again with a tissue. 'I'm so sorry, Henry. I wish I had more to tell you.'

'You're doing just fine, Abby girl.' He bent low, took the small woman in his arms, and kissed her gently on the forehead. Giving her a brave smile, he said, 'We must have faith that God will keep them safe.'

He composed himself, took in a deep breath, and returned to his seat. It was his fault his wife and son were missing. He had sent them to Texas for a republican party fundraiser. Because of it, they both might be dead. He closed his eyes tightly to block out the thought. He had told Abby to keep it together, and he needed to do the same.

He stood to address the men and women gathered before him. 'If I could have your attention, please.'

The murmuring in the room was silenced, and the president took a deep breath. The lump in his throat felt like it would choke him. 'First, I would like to hear from ...,' he paused to look at his notes, 'Dr. Matthew Lawrence.'

Dr. Lawrence stood and took his place before the room. 'I am Dr. Lawrence, Mr. President.'

Blinking his eyes slowly, the president tried to gather his thoughts before he returned his gaze to the man standing before him. 'It is my understanding, Dr. Lawrence, that you are a world-renowned volcanologist. Please provide us with as much information as possible concerning what took place this morning at Yellowstone.'

'Mr. President, I hope you will bear with me whenever I make statements that are obvious facts since I am uncertain how much those in attendance know about the study of volcanos. At the moment, we do know there was an earthquake measuring 11.9 on the Richter Scale that occurred at 0740 Mountain Time Zone in Yellowstone National Park.'

There were several gasps of alarm.

Dr. Lawrence held up his hand to quiet the crowd and continued. 'This caused an eruption.' He bowed his head to rethink his statement. 'No. That is actually incorrect, sir. It caused what is known as a *super eruption* at the ...'

Admiral Stockton interrupted. 'What is the difference between an eruption and a super eruption, Dr. Lawrence?'

He licked his dry lips before continuing. 'A super eruption is several thousand times more powerful than a normal eruption, sir. The two can hardly be compared.'

The admiral grunted. 'And what makes you think this is not just an ordinary eruption like the ones that occur in the Hawaiian Islands from time to time?'

Dr. Lawrence stared hard at Admiral Stockton. 'Because I felt it here in Washington D.C., sir. I am sure you did, too. Driving here, I saw broken windows in hundreds of homes and office buildings. A normal eruption from 1760 miles away would not have done that. I have also been informed the electrical grid and communication towers for the entire United States are down and why we are using generators in the White House. The eruption column rose over 330,000 feet into our atmosphere, well over 60 miles, in case you were wondering, as recorded by NASA. Mount St. Helen's, by comparison, rose 80,000 feet. Should I continue, Admiral Stockton?'

President Holder held up his hand to calm the two gentlemen. 'Please, Dr. Lawrence. Tell us your best estimate of what we can expect in the days ahead.'

Dr. Lawrence took in a deep breath. 'Mr. President, the last time Yellowstone had a super eruption was almost 700,000 years ago. Contemporary science has proven super eruptions have occurred only three times in human history at Yellowstone. My best estimation is that we may be ...' He paused and looked around the room. 'This could very well be an extinction event, sir, affecting the entire planet. No one is safe. The devastation and loss of life will be incomprehensible. We are facing what is called a *nuclear winter*: the next ice age. What I mean by that, Mr. President, is this super eruption is currently spewing millions of tons of sulfuric acid, volcanic gases, and ash into our atmosphere. The ash will block out the sunlight for months, perhaps years, causing all plant life and animals to die. There will be mass starvation.' He wiped his forehead before continuing. 'That is my best estimation, sir.'

Jumping to his feet with an expression of rage written across his face, Admiral Stockton addressed the president. 'This man,' he pointed a shaking finger at Dr. Lawrence, 'is an alarmist, Mr. President. There is no way he can know what events we are facing. I, for one, refuse to accept his statements as fact.'

Arching his eyebrows, Dr. Lawrence retorted. 'You may come to find in the days ahead of us that you have no alternative in this matter, Admiral. With that said, Mr. President, you have some of the finest, most brilliant minds in the United States sitting in this audience. Please ask for other opinions, sir.'

The president rose before the group. 'I would appreciate hearing from someone else.'

Several men and two women took to their feet. He nodded at one of the women. 'Your name, please?'

'My name is Dr. Patricia Sanders, Mr. President. I am a scientist and a mathematician. I would like to say that I have known Dr. Lawrence for nearly 30 years, and he is certainly not an alarmist. My second point is if this morning's earthquake measuring 11.9 on the Richter Scale is accurate, it would make it the world's largest earthquake recorded since accurate readings became possible. It has been hypothesized that an earthquake measuring at 10.0 would release the energy of twice the estimated yield of the world's stockpiled nuclear weapons; a 15.0 on the Richter Scale would rip the planet apart. You can see, sir, if Wyoming experienced an 11.9 this morning, followed by a super eruption as Dr. Lawrence stated, then God help us. There will be millions of casualties with many more to follow.'

* * *

The White House aide stood in the darkened hallway outside of the Oval Office, contemplating all she had heard in the meeting. The emergency lights flickered like they do in horror films, casting ominous shadows on the walls. President Holder had been informed the two attempts made by the U.S. Air Force to photograph the west coast had met with disastrous failure. The two aircrews, with a total of 17 men on board, had gone down – all airmen presumed dead. The cause of both crashes was the direct result of the massive ash cloud from the Yellowstone eruption; the ash cloud covering the entire west coast was making its way eastward and nothing could stop it. The mood in the Oval Office was one of complete despair. If the most powerful man alive had lost hope ... she shook her head as if to clear it. *No, there was always hope – her parents and the church told her so.* The aide glanced down at the hunched-over figure of the broken man seated in the waiting area ... waiting to be escorted into the Oval Office.

'Administrator Adams, the president will see you now.' When no reply was forthcoming, she lightly touched his shoulder.

Startled from his thoughts, George jumped at her touch only to be surprised to see a young, attractive woman in a tightly pressed, dark blue pantsuit standing in front of him.

'Yes?' he stammered. 'What is it?'

A wave of sadness washed over her. She saw his eyes were swollen from crying. 'The president will see you now, sir.'

George slowly got to his feet and ran both of his hands though his thinning hair. He wiped his eyes in embarrassment and straightened his tie. With a deep sigh, he entered the Oval Office without knocking. He was quite sure it would be his last visit to the White House.

* * *

President Holder and National Security Advisor O'Henry were both seated on the same leather sofa. Across from them sat Vice President Timmons, Admiral Stockton, and General Sterling. Ms. Fitzgerald and CDC Director Roberts were both seated behind the president's desk.

George could hardly look at the president's face. The man seemed to have aged ten years since the briefing room meeting less than an hour ago. An almost-empty bottle of cognac sat on an antique silver tray in front of them, and from the looks of things, it was not their first bottle. Given the present circumstances, he was not the least bit surprised.

The president set his eyes upon George; his face was swollen and red-blotched from the brandy. It was a look that George knew too well. His words were slurred. 'George, I understand you have more information for us concerning the west coast. What is it?'

He took in the faces of the people seated in front of him. President Holder was the only one interested in what he had to say. The others seemed to be lost in their own thoughts. George cleared his throat, wishing he had a sip of the brandy. 'There have been two more major earthquakes, Mr. President. The first one measured 10.2 on the Richter Scale, with its epicenter along the San Andreas Fault. The second earthquake measured 9.7 along the Texas border with Mexico. There is currently no word on casualties or damage, sir. Dr. Sanders and Dr. Lawrence have both stated we can expect these earthquakes to not only continue, but drastically increase in severity over time.'

The president gave a wan nod. 'Do you have any word on my wife and son yet, George? Did their plane land safely?'

He shifted uneasily. 'No word at this time, sir. Several planes did make safe landings immediately following the eruption. Some in fields and some on major highways.' He bit his lip. 'I'm sorry to say, sir, but most of the aircraft in the air during the eruption crashed due to mechanical failure from the volcanic ash clogging the engines.' He stared down at his feet. 'I am sure your wife and son's plane made a safe landing, sir.'

Managing a weak smile, he thanked the administrator and said, 'George, I have faith God will keep them safe.'

Marjorie's computer beeped. The screen in front of her flashed a weak amber color, and she read quietly what was written before her. 'Henry,' her voice was hoarse. 'The commercial plane the fighter jet shot down ...' Her face was deathly pale. 'The bodies washed up along the New Jersey and New York shoreline.

All emergency crews and medical personnel are showing signs of the plague.' She was unable to continue and teetered for a second. Her eyes rolled back in her head, and she collapsed onto the floor.

* * *

Navy Captain, Dr. Dennis White looked into the eyes of the president kneeling next to him. 'I'm very sorry, sir. She's gone.'

The president took her small hand in his and kissed it gently. 'Oh, Maggie.'

Outside, gray ash started to fall onto the American flags flying proudly around the Washington Monument.

* * *

George followed closely behind the gurney transporting Marjorie's body into the West Wing corridor. The two orderlies pushed her stretcher down the hallway, past the elevator, and to the stairwell door. *Elevators are now a thing of the past, forever buried.* He wondered despairingly how many people were aware of that fact.

'It's all falling apart, isn't it, Mr. Adams?'

George turned to see Marine General Sterling standing next to him. Even in the darkness of the hallway, he could see the expression of sorrow on the proud Marine's face. 'I'm sorry, General. What was that?'

'I asked you if it's all falling apart. From what I have heard since this morning, the west coast of the United States is gone while the plague is spreading unchecked across Europe and Asia. A friend of mine stationed in Germany said bodies are being left wherever they fall. Were you aware of that, Mr. Adams?' General Sterling did not wait for a reply. 'The plague has reached our shores; Dr. Roberts said that there is no cure, and I believe her. God rest her soul. For the first time in my life, I am happy to have no family, which is why I asked you: is it all falling apart?'

He ignored the question and glanced toward the Oval Office. 'How is President Holder doing, General?'

The general's face hardened. 'The president has ordered me, along with the vice president and national security advisor, to leave immediately for the Pentagon. He will remain here at the White House with Admiral Stockton. He asked for a moment of privacy.' The general turned on his heel to leave but stopped and faced George one last time. 'You know that his wife and son are dead, don't you, Mr. Adams?'

George cast his eyes downward. 'I don't know that, sir.'

'I think you do know, Mr. Adams. Yes, I think you do.'

* * *

George quit pacing and took a seat in the West Wing corridor once again. It had been nearly forty minutes since his conversation with General Sterling, and his hands were still shaking. *How had Sterling known?*

The door leading into the Oval Office remained closed since the vice president and his party left for the Pentagon, and he had seen no one since then. He covered his eyes with both hands. General Sterling had been right. It was falling apart, and it would happen faster than anyone could imagine. He had started to pace the hallway once more when the sound of a gunshot came from inside the Oval Office. The unusual loudness within the confines of the White House caused him to stagger against the wall. A Secret Service agent rushed past him, down the richly carpeted corridor, followed closely by a Marine captain. Both men had their handguns drawn. The door leading into the Oval Office was unlocked when the two men arrived.

Admiral Stockton was standing over the lifeless body of President Henry R. Holder, and he was still holding his .45 caliber handgun. The men stared at the admiral in disbelief. He looked at each of them in turn with tears running down his face. 'The president ordered me to do him this one last favor. His family's plane went down just outside of the Dallas Airport. His wife and son are both dead. How could I refuse him? How could I?' He put the barrel of his weapon against the side of his head, saluted the Marine captain, and pulled the trigger.

* * *

'*It's all falling apart, isn't it, Mr. Adams?*' George sat up slowly. His head was throbbing, and every movement he made was painful. He was back at his apartment, in his own bed. It had all been nothing more than a bad dream, a nightmare. He shook his head to clear the cobwebs and a fresh wave of pain shot across his forehead. He spilled the drink he had been holding and cursed himself. He had fallen asleep with a shot glass full of whiskey in his hand and was still dressed in the suit he had worn to the White House. It had not been a bad dream after all. He fumbled for the switch to his table lamp and turned it on. Nothing. No power. His clock next to his bedside read 11:32 P.M. *Why is the clock working and not the lamp? Batteries, you idiot. The clock runs on batteries.* He rolled over onto his stomach and reached underneath the bed. *My flashlight is around here somewhere. Ah, there it is.* He turned it on and swept the light around his bedroom. There was a small bottle of cognac on the bedside table, but it was not his brand. This bottle was well outside of his price range. He suddenly remembered everything: President Holder was dead, shot by one of his closest friends, Admiral Stockton – a mercy killing and suicide.

He ran his hand over his forehead. He was drenched in sweat. *How long had he been out for?* He got out of bed and went into the bathroom. The reflection looking back at him from the mirror was one he barely recognized. He splashed cold water against his face and over his head.

They were *dead*. Killed during takeoff in Dallas. President Holder blamed himself for their deaths, which is why he asked the admiral to kill him. The entire world was falling apart, and he had answered the call by getting drunk from the brandy he had stolen from the Oval Office.

He looked out his bedroom window at the city below him. It was pitch black outside: no streetlights. *Nothing.* No light anywhere. He could see ash on the window sill; he opened his window and stuck out his hand. Within seconds, his hand was covered in large gray flakes mixed with tiny bits of ground-up rock. He closed the window, walked back into his bathroom, and looked closely at the ash under the bright light of his flashlight.

Anyone outside would be breathing this crap in. He washed his hands and watched as the ash circled the drain, leaving several small pieces of rock behind. He wiped them up with a tissue and flushed it down the toilet. *No one could breathe that shit in and hope to live long. It would build up in the lungs like wet cement. What could he do? What could anyone do?*

He opened the medicine cabinet and took out two sleeping pills. He refused to think about it anymore and just wanted – *needed* – to sleep. He went back to his bed, poured himself another shot of cognac, and washed down the two pills. Emptying the glass, he poured himself another.

He opened his nightstand drawer, took out a large candle, and lit it. *God, how he hated the dark.* There were hidden things lurking in the shadows and in the closet, waiting for him to fall asleep. He knew it was an irrational fear from his childhood, but he could not shake the thought from his mind. He laid down in his bed and covered himself with the sheet. The flame from the candle made shadows come alive on the walls; he closed his eyes to block them out, and soon, was fast asleep.

* * *

The visions came to him, and he knew they were true. Jesus Christ promised retribution as he hung from the cross ... and the time had come.

He saw a great earthquake splitting the west coast apart and awakening Yellowstone from its long slumber. He saw the bloated bodies of plague victims lying in the streets wherever they had fallen. He saw the rats and the birds carrying the disease to every corner of the earth. Man turning on man until no one was left.

He thrashed in his sleep, trying to ward off the sight of it all. There really were things waiting in the dark. His hand knocked the candle off the night stand and onto the carpet. George's worries were almost at an end ...

TWENTY-EIGHT

ATLANTIC CITY, NEW JERSEY.

September 27, 2030.

The man sat on the boardwalk, watching the slow rise and fall of the ocean's swell. High overhead, a lone seagull cried, and he raised his eyes to watch it circle in the gloomy darkness above him. Falling gray ash dusted his clothing and hair, but he noticed none of it.

The man and his wife had driven over 1200 miles to the Jersey shore from their home in Pine Bluff, Arkansas, two days ago on the *trip of a lifetime*. They learned of the Yellowstone eruption when they arrived in New Jersey; they had escaped the eruption only to find they faced a plague.

The man glanced backward, away from the ocean. He stared at the casino where his wife laid in eternal sleep. She had fallen ill shortly after their arrival at the hotel. There were few people to be seen anywhere, except for some hotel staff and a few guests when they checked in. The electricity was out across the country, but the hotel was running on generator power. The concierge, bellhop, and people they passed on the stairs on their way up to their room were all coughing. He had tipped the bellhop a generous $3 and joked he would earn his money with the elevator being without power. His wife had died in bed, a scant seven hours after their arrival. She said she felt feverish and was having trouble breathing. He ran downstairs to the lobby to find help, but the few people he had come across were already dead or close to it. Some had died at the blackjack and roulette tables, still clutching their money. Hurrying back to their room, he found his wife was dead. She was lying halfway out of their bed; her right hand reaching out. For what, he did not know. He had gotten her back onto the bed and held her in his arms, praying for her sickness to take him.

The man returned his gaze to the ocean. A bitter breeze blew the gray ash across the sand. He glanced along the boardwalk to his right and saw dozens of corpses lying in the ash; seagulls picking at their flesh. To his left, he saw a woman sitting alone, just as he was. The woman's purse was open, and the wind was blowing its contents across the boardwalk and along the beach; she made no attempt to gather any of it.

He got up and walked toward the ocean. He was a Christian man, a man of God, and a man of faith. He abhorred the idea of suicide, so he lied to himself and said he was only taking a swim to wash his body of the ash. He undressed, folded his clothes neatly, and left the pile on the shoreline. The water was frigid but bearable. He eventually reached a point of no return and treaded water. He took one last look at the hotel where he left his dear wife. Without a second thought, he faced the horizon and started to swim once more...

TWENTY-NINE

MANHATTAN, NEW YORK CITY, NEW YORK.

October 2, 2030.

He had been listening to the sound of gunfire on the streets below his apartment for several hours. In the semidarkness, Robert knew the twilight was no longer temporary – there would be no more sunlight for years to come.

Cotton, a curled-up ball of black and white fur, was sound asleep next to him, snoring contently. His wristwatch flashed 7:32 A.M. On a normal day, he would be in the kitchen preparing breakfast. Ever since the Yellowstone eruption on September 26th and the plague infecting the entire east coast, *normal* no longer existed.

Word on the street was that once you were infected with the disease, you had less than 24 hours to live, but who knew the truth anymore? Everything was gone: newspapers, television, the Internet. According to rumor, anything west of the Mississippi River no longer existed for any practical purpose, a proverbial wasteland – even the farm belt that supplied most of the food for America was covered in over eight feet of ash and pumice.

He poured himself a glass of rye and swallowed it. His daughter and his ex-wife, living in California, were dead. He wiped his eyes with the back of his hand and poured himself another drink. It was his fault they moved out west. *If only he had been more of a man.* He shook his head, hoping to force the memory from his mind.

Millions of Americans were supposedly dead as a result of the initial blast from the super volcano; millions more were soon to follow. Starvation, the plague, or the effects of the *nuclear winter* was expected to kill them all.

Humanity was doing quite a number on its own kind, too. Gunfire and screams of the dying permeated the air of New York City, and it was going to get a lot fucking worse.

Electricity and all forms of communication ceased shortly after the eruption. He was grateful to receive no more phone calls from the N.Y.P.D. begging him to report to work. Most likely, his fellow officers were not reporting for duty, either. They were probably hunkered down in their homes trying to protect their families from roving gangs or others driven to violence in search of food ... or they were dead. There would be no surviving what was taking place in the United States, or the whole planet, for that matter. To venture outside risked exposure to the plague or fellow man, both equally deadly.

He had been having the same dream every night for months: raging storms, Yellowstone National Park erupting, and rats and birds carrying the plague to every corner of the planet. Mother Nature was a badass bitch, and she was pissed off. There would be no end to the storms, no cure for the plague, and no satisfying the rats' hunger.

Robert was no longer afraid of Hell, for Hell had come to earth, and it planned to stay around for a long, long time.

* * *

His bedroom window was covered in ash; the gray powder was falling heavily over the city. It arrived in N.Y.C. less than twenty hours after the eruption, covering the entire city in its hot embrace. From his apartment's vantage point, it appeared that the ash blanket on the ground was at least two feet thick.

He recalled a show he had seen about the effects of a *nuclear winter.* The various scientists all shared the same opinion: the sulfuric gases released during the eruption would rise into the atmosphere, mix with the planet's water vapor, and block all sunlight. Without sunlight, the massive drop in temperature across the planet would create a worldwide food shortage.

He opened his window and held out his hand, catching the gritty ash in his palm. He leaned out his window for a better look at the ruins below him and saw bodies everywhere.

With disgust, he closed his window and slumped down into his favorite chair. There was nothing that could be done for the dead. Nothing at all.

Robert had no desire to stick around and watch the latest events unfold. He wasn't being a coward, just sensible. His small stockpile of food and water was already running low, and the water coming out of the sink's tap was putrid and brown. Even the so-called *doomsday preppers* hiding underground in their bunkers would run out of food and water, eventually. If they even survived a year or two, what was the point?

* * *

Getting up from his chair, he trudged into his bathroom in a trance. His reflection in the mirror claimed his thoughts and replayed old memories he was never meant to return to. *Most of us forget the memories that were most special to us; yet, we remember the nightmares that haunt our dreams forever.*

He opened his medicine cabinet and grabbed the Nembutal off the top shelf. Walking into the kitchen with his bottle of pills, he looked at every item he had set out the night before on the table, waiting for him: a cat dish, the cat food, his service weapon, and a bottle of whiskey. He opened all the capsules one-by-one and emptied the powder into a bowl. He mixed some of the drug into the bag of cat food and emptied the remainder into a shot glass filled with some of his best whiskey.

Cotton sauntered into the kitchen, drawn there by the sound of his breakfast being prepared, and rubbed his body along Robert's leg until he picked him up. Stroking the cat's back and rubbing under his chin, he felt more love for the tiny creature than anything left in his life.

The poison will cause Cotton too much pain. Cradling the furball in one arm, he snatched up his shot of whiskey and his service weapon. Making one last trip into his bedroom with everything he needed, he laid down on his bed. The cat nuzzled his head against Robert's chest, purring loudly. In one smooth motion, he snapped the cat's neck with his hands. 'I'm so damn sorry, little Cotton.' Hot tears poured down his cheeks as he picked up the shot glass and drank it all in one quick gulp. The pain was immediate.

Taking his service weapon from its holster, he put the barrel into his mouth, tilted it upward, and pulled the trigger.

On the streets below, streets Robert Gray had walked many a beat on, the gray ash continued to fall.

THIRTY

NEW YORK CITY, NEW YORK.

October 7, 2030.

New York City was eerily silent, save for the occasional gunshot or the sound of breaking glass. The falling ash and thick layer of pumice absorbed the sounds of the city like a dry sponge soaking up water. All traffic had ceased; abandoned cars lined every street as far as the eye could see. Fires burned out of control in all directions – building after building set ablaze by roving gangs sat unattended, burning silently to the ground – no longer rescued by fire departments. In fact, there were no firetruck alarms, no police sirens, and no warbling ambulances to indicate assistance was on its way; signs of compassion and hope were a thing of the past. People were either gone, hiding, or dead.

* * *

The Metropolitan Museum of Art and the American Museum of Natural History were up in flames; their fires started by a career pyromaniac with nothing more than a book of wooden matches and a small can of gasoline.

In the Metropolitan Museum of Art, Benjamin D. Miller clutched his gas can in one hand and a bottle of rum in the other; he stood paralyzed in fascination as room after room of priceless

167

works of art dripped paint down their walls, creating their own masterpieces. The destroyer delighted in becoming the master.

With the artwork in ruins, he continued his fiery adventure at the American Museum of Natural History, specifically in the Hall of North American Mammals. He took great pleasure in breaking the glass of each individual exhibit and lighting the animals on fire. Satisfied, he sat down on a bench in the great hall to admire his handiwork and watch the deer, goats, and brown bears burn; however, the taxidermy chemicals mixed with carbon dioxide had their own agenda. Ben was lulled into an eternal sleep ... the destroyed had enacted its own revenge.

* * *

With the complete lack of police presence, two serial rapists and killers, Simon J. Brown and longtime friend, Alex Vernon, were on the prowl again. Violently raping and slashing the throats of two females only a few hours earlier had increased their appetite for more, and they had their eyes set on their third victim. She was a young twenty-something blond who lived alone in her brownstone home with her small yapping dog.

Brown, who was an expert locksmith, used his handy trade whenever the men had the *urge* to force themselves on any woman they fancied. Their latest target was marked, and they made their move.

The two men easily picked the bolt to the backdoor of the young woman's house, but the small yapping dog had alerted their soon-to-be victim. Fleeing to her bedroom, she locked herself inside. The chase heightened their desires; they knew the girl's bedroom door was no match for them, but the business-end of the twelve-gauge shotgun the young blonde was aiming at them sure was.

* * *

At the corner of 5th Avenue and East 65th Street, two homeless men with violent pasts and a runaway teen were standing beneath a bus awning, thrilled with the amount of alcohol they had pilfered from the R&J Liquor store before breakfast. While in a deep discussion on which business they would hit next, the wealthy, well-dressed eighty-two-year-old gentleman, Devon B. Whitman, suffering from hearing loss and Alzheimer's crossed their paths on his way to nowhere. Known for wearing a Rolex and several diamond rings, he quickly caught the attention of the three men. As Mr. Whitman strolled by them, one of the homeless men hit him from behind with a crowbar, bashing in his skull and knocking him to the sidewalk. Seeing the older man was somehow still alive, the teenager grabbed the bar and finished him off, ending his suffering. Stealing his jewelry and wallet, it never occurred to any of them that money and jewels were obsolete in this new world.

***

While Mr. Whitman and many others lay dead on the sidewalks, the animals at the Central Park Zoo had their own horrific fate – none of them had been cared for since the 2nd of October. Those housed alone in their habitats had succumbed to dehydration and starvation. Animals living in colonies or packs had turned on each other as a means of survival ... a preview of what was to come for humanity.

THIRTY-ONE

THE PINE BARRENS, NEW JERSEY.

November 10, 2030.

The highway stretched endlessly in front of him. He staggered on, putting one foot in front of the other. Both of his legs felt weak, and his left calf had gone numb. He knew he would have to rest soon, if only for a few minutes. He sat down on the bumper of the nearest car, a Ford Escape from the look of it, but it was hard to tell under all the ash covering it. He lifted his wrist and looked at his watch. Before the eruption, he was a wealthy Wall Street broker, and the solid-gold watch he was staring at had cost him $30,000. The GPS no longer worked, but the temperature gauge did, and it was measuring 8 °F. He got to his feet with difficulty and plodded slowly through the dark gray ash.

He needed to keep moving; every step brought him closer to his destination. *What was that destination?* He neither remembered nor cared. The bitter cold and constant hunger had numbed his senses. He eventually recalled the sign he had seen nailed to a tree several days ago. *What day of the week had it been when he came across that sign? Doesn't matter.*

SETTLEMENT. CAPE MAY, N.J.
MAKE YOUR WAY THERE: FOOD. WATER. SHELTER.
TAKE GARDEN STATE PARKWAY SOUTH.
PARKWAY IS BLOCKED.
WALK OR RIDE BIKE. GOOD LUCK.

At the time, the sign had been partially buried in dead, colorless weeds and gray ash that fell incessantly from a sky he could no longer see. Why he had felt the need to unbury the sign, he could not recall. The bright lights, music, crowds, fine foods and good drink were all gone ... dead, including any hope. Except for that sign he had discovered: an inkling of hope. *What if it was a hoax? Someone's idea of a bad joke? A trap?* That horrible thought stopped him in his tracks, making him tremble in fear. He thought of the hooded black-cloaked men he had seen on the road and in the woods. He reached into his coat pocket and withdrew the Colt .38 Special revolver. Removing his glove, he opened the cylinder. Only one round was left. *How could that be?* Yesterday, *or had it been the day before*, he had taken several shots at a rabbit and missed. He finally dismissed all the negative thoughts. He had to have hope ... it was all he had left.

Cape May, New Jersey. He had been there once, maybe twice. He looked forward to seeing the ocean and perhaps even some beautiful women. *Was there any beauty left in this broken world for him to see?* He could not answer the question because he was afraid of the answer. *What if he was the only man left? That wasn't possible, was it? No, of course not.* Others were still out there somewhere. He had seen their tracks in the ash and their campfires at night: the shrouded ones. He came across one of their campsites after they had moved on. They always traveled in packs, like animals, and he was sure they were looking for him. *Was he becoming paranoid?* His thoughts returned to the campsite he stumbled upon. He was hoping to find a small bite of food left behind on the campfire, but all he saw were very small bones and a child's ripped and blood-stained clothing. *Dear God. How could they have done this? How could anyone do something so inhuman?* There was no point in continuing to think about what he had found.

He started walking again, focusing his mind and hope on Cape May. The parkway was indeed blocked with abandoned cars, semitrailers, and tour buses heading toward Atlantic City, just as the sign nailed to the tree stated. He opened the door to a nearby camper, hoping to forage some food or water, perhaps even find another gun to use for hunting and self-protection. The smell of death greeted him. A grinning corpse sat behind the steering wheel while several more were piled on the floor: an entire family of dead, bloated bodies. He quickly shut the door and threw up what little there was in his stomach. He continued walking with zero intention of opening any more car doors. It had been several miles before he came upon another camper that had run off the highway, crashed into a tree, and flipped onto its side. What caught his attention was the men's ten-speed bicycle strapped to the back of the camper. He untied the straps and lowered the bike to the ground. It was in perfect condition with twin pouches mounted behind the seat. His hands fumbled as he untied the snaps of each pouch. He found several bags of beef jerky and potato chips. There was even a chocolate bar. *Treasure!* Not all hope was lost.

He sat down on the rear bumper of a minivan and said a quick prayer of thanks. He finished a package of jerky in a matter of minutes. *When was the last time he had eaten?* He put the pouches back on the bike and mounted it with care. He started off slowly; his legs were unaccustomed to the movement as he weaved his way between cars and trucks.

The hours and miles passed by steadily, and in time, he saw a highway sign stating he was entering the Pine Barrens; Cape May was in sixty miles. In the northbound lane, he saw movement. His mind told him to ride away and hide – the shrouded ones were coming for him, but it looked like two teenage boys. He waved and called out to them, but they darted into the woods. Afraid of his intentions, no doubt. *So, he was not the only one left alive.*

Night was upon him, and the cold wind and ash were swirling about, making it difficult to see. His watch showed the temperature was hovering around 2 °F; the two heavy coats he always wore were doing little to protect him from the bitterness. He eased the bicycle down a steep embankment to a sheltered area and began to build a simple campsite. Below him, off to the right, he noticed a stream bed that had long since frozen over. If he could break through the ice, there might be water or even a fish to cook.

He took his time edging his way down the slope, holding onto tree branches along the way to steady his descent. He found a spot near the shoreline where the ice was not too thick and began to chip away at it, praying the sound would not carry too far. Brackish water rose to the surface – enough to boil.

He started back up the slope, working his way again from one branch to the next for balance. He was almost to his campsite when one of the branches broke under his weight. Slipping, he made a desperate grab for another branch, but it was dead and broke off in his hand. He fell backward, and his right foot got caught between two large rocks. Something snapped in his ankle, and he screamed in agony. He carefully touched his swollen ankle and felt a dampness spreading; the bone had broken through the skin. Nausea washed over him, his vision wavered, and he blacked out. When he came to, he was staring up at the falling ash.

'I'm going to die here.' The sound of his own voice and the words he had spoken scared him. He prayed with all he had for God to help him and not let him freeze to death in this lonely place. He thought about his mother and father who had died last year when a twister struck their farmhouse. Knowing he would see them soon was comforting.

He heard a noise in the brush behind him, and the fear of what it might be took his breath away. He craned his neck as far as possible to see what was moving nearby. It was a small dog: a Beagle. He whistled to it, but it sat and stared at him. He heard more branches snapping, and a Doberman Pinscher stepped into view, flanked by two more Dobermans and a German Shepherd. The German Shepherd made a low guttural noise and bared its teeth.

He withdrew his .38 Special with its last remaining round. He knew it was hopeless, but he prayed the noise would at least scare them away. He fired and thought he had hit one of the Dobermans. The dogs ran off into the dense brush; he laid back down on the grass and let out a sigh of relief. He attempted to crawl back up the slope ... if he could reach his camp, he could clean his wound. *There might still be a chance.*

He heard the thick brush snapping around him once again. The stray dogs had returned and brought others with them. God had indeed answered his prayer; he was not going to freeze to death after all...

THIRTY-TWO

GREENSBORO, NORTH CAROLINA.

December 7, 2030.

In the valley below her, she thought she spotted a red barn. The continuously falling black soot was disorienting – the hideous snowflakes covered every aspect of life, making the world a dirty gray color. *When was the last time that she had felt the sun on her face, gazed at the moon, or seen the stars?* Her memory of the past was fading at an alarming rate. *This should not be happening; I am only nineteen.* She had not seen her reflection in a mirror for so long she was unsure if she would even recognize her own face.

Would she live long enough to see anything worthwhile again? Would she still be alive tomorrow?

As the temperature declined and snow mixed with the ash, her fingertips and toes felt like ice – her gloves and heavy socks were of no use anymore. She had to find shelter soon. *The red barn.* It did not look too far from where she stood; although, she knew from her father's teachings that distance could be deceiving. Memories of her father filled her with sadness. The plague had killed him within hours, and she was left on her own in the bleakness. *Why is God allowing this to happen to His children?*

Her descent into the valley was even more treacherous with the cold wind whipping around her. A noise to her left startled her, and she lost her footing, causing her to plop down hard onto the gray slush. The sight of a small rabbit skirting around the brush caused her stomach to rumble.

When had she last eaten? She had never killed one of God's creatures before, not even a bug, and would not kill anything for her own survival. She still had a few precious items in her backpack: half a loaf of hard bread, some stale cheese, several cans of soup, and chocolate bars she had found in the backseat of an abandoned car. *Why have I not eaten any of my meager supplies? I need to save them for when I am really hungry, for when my stomach starts to eat away from within.* She recalled she *had* eaten yesterday morning because she promised herself to eat daily. She smiled at the thought of being safely inside the barn with a small fire, eating hot soup, bread, and cheese. Getting to her feet, she brushed herself off and carefully made her way down the hillside.

Her father was a woodsman and taught her survival tactics: building a fire, seeking shelter, boiling water for drinking, and hunting for food. Thinking again of her father caused her to stop in her tracks. If the plague killed him, why did she survive? She leaned against a huge pine tree, hot tears coursing down her cheeks.

'I miss you so much, Daddy.'

She wiped her face and nose on her sleeve; it would do no good to cry at this temperature.

The crevices of the rocky bluffs above her made an eerie howling sound as the wind whipped through, sending a shiver down her spine. Alone and vulnerable in the freezing elements, she refocused on the barn; twenty minutes later, she was standing at the gate of the fenced-in pasture. Several bleached-white animal skeletons littered the ground within the enclosure. *Sheep, maybe?* To the right of the barn were the ruins of a burned-down farmhouse she had not noticed earlier.

She crouched, hiding herself until she could ascertain the area was deserted. *They* were out there somewhere: the men in black cloaks who kept their faces covered. They were hunting her and had been for several days. One night while using the massive branches of a huge oak tree as a safe place to sleep, the men wearing cloaks passed beneath her. It was the only time she was grateful for the never-ending ash because it covered her tracks and hid her well. She had not seen them up-close before, and the sight of them scared her, but it was their conversation that flooded her body and soul with dread. They discussed the vile things they wanted to do to her in gory detail: beginning with rape and ending with a feast of her flesh.

She stood up and edged toward the barn, being careful not to step on any ice or branches. She circled the perimeter, listening closely for any subtle sounds of life. *Nothing*. Holding her breath, she opened the barndoor – empty. Dense cobwebs filled the entrance, and no footprints were imprinted on the damp earth. She selected a stall with the most bedding and set about kindling a small fire. Her mouth was watering in anticipation of warm food filling her belly.

* * *

After licking her fingers clean of any remaining crumbs, she unrolled her blanket and said prayers for her mother who died in childbirth, her father, those still alive in this shattered world, and herself. Within minutes of finishing, she was sound asleep. Outside, the barren land and thin boards of the red barn were no match for the temperature drop; her small fire died a quick death at -47 °F.

The shrouded ones discovered her frozen body four days later. She was beyond satisfying their carnal desires, but a few turns on a fire spit satisfied their feeding ...

THIRTY-THREE

CAMINO DE SANTIAGO, SPAIN.

December 30, 2030.

They were all dead ... every one of his brothers in the monastery were dead. The plague-yielding rats had done their job well. Some of his fellow monks fled the confines of the monastery, praying for some miracle to save them in the outside world. Ironically, departing the monastery would most certainly lead to death – there was nothing for them beyond the ancient walls except starvation, disease, and the rats.

From his bedroom window, he longingly gazed at his grandmother's oak tree. God's punishment of man was almost at an end, and his prayer for eternal damnation for all had been answered. Without a backward glance, he walked out of his room for the final time. The hallways of the monastery were dark and empty; his footsteps echoed loudly as he made his way down the wooden stairwell to the front door and stepped outside for the first time in seventy-seven years. Against the moss-covered old wall was a ladder the gardeners had left behind. He struggled to move the ladder, but he continued until he had it leaning against the ancient tree. Caressing the bark of the tree like that of a lover, he knew his time had come. Like his grandmother, the tree would be his Golgotha – his execution site. He climbed the ladder, swung a rope around the strongest branch, and secured it tightly. Fastening the rope around his neck, he looked to the sky one last time. Gray ash blanketed his face as Eberhardt stepped into oblivion.

THIRTY-FOUR

GREAT BEAR LAKE, CANADA.

January 28, 2031.

Rattled from a nightmare by an unrecognizable sound, he bolted upright only to have a piercing pain in his head force him back to the ground. He touched his scalp ... it was caked in dried blood. *How did that happen?* The frigid darkness brought him back to his dream.

* * *

He and his wife were stumbling through the woods like blind men – the blackness of the night, impenetrable. While holding each other's hand for comfort and safety, they each extended their opposite hand in a vain attempt to protect their faces from a wayward tree branch. Along the way, they discussed the past and taking basic needs like food, water, and simple streetlights for granted. They talked about the future of their two children; she grabbed both of his hands in hers and begged him to flee with the family to a safer place. He assured her their safety was his utmost concern, and that they were fully prepared for handling any situation. The stockpile of food, water, guns, and ammo in their basement bunker would keep them safe for years. Unfortunately, they were not safe, and his wife and children were dead. He anticipated natural disasters and economic collapse; however, nothing could shield them from an incurable plague sweeping across the planet with a mortality rate of 99 percent: a disease he was immune to, somehow, but the rest of his family was not.

* * *

A harsh, scraping sound brought him back to the present. There was a trapdoor being moved above him. The shrouded ones were keeping him as a prisoner and were lowering food down to him ... food, *if you could even call it that*: stale bread, a small bite of cheese, and a tin cup with foul-tasting water. *How long had he been in this hole? One day, perhaps two. It was impossible to tell anymore.* He ate his moldy cheese out of necessity. The trapdoor snapped shut; all light faded. Alone in the bone-numbing dank pit, he felt his way along the dirt floor to the corner of his Hell. *He was being kept captive in a hole in the ground like some animal awaiting its slaughter.* From what he had been able to see in the dim light cast by their fire above the hatch, there were wooden beams crossing the ceiling at least ten feet above him – no way to escape, and the slick walls contained no hand holds to crawl out to safety. He laid down on the floor and gathered whatever debris he could find around him for warmth. Something slithered across his bare leg, and he recoiled in revulsion. *Had it been a centipede or a scorpion?* His imagination was running rampant. He tried to sleep, and did for a time, then the sound of the trapdoor opening again startled him. Looking up, he saw three men staring down at him; their features always hidden by their cloaks. A ladder was lowered into the pit, and he was ordered to climb out. Fear gripped his mind; all hope was lost, and death was near.

Finally, above ground, he saw night was still upon them, but the immediate area was lit up brightly by a roaring fire licking the edges of a huge hole in the ground. Several men, shrouded in black, standing nearby were illuminated like demons by the flickering flames. His wrists were bound tightly behind his back before he was shoved to the ground. A thin, deathly pale woman approached him with her eyes downcast. She poked at his ribs and lifted his chin with her filthy hand crusted black and cracked from the cold. Her satisfied smile was filled with brown, pitted teeth and rancid breath. The long knife she withdrew from its sheath strapped to her waist glinted in the firelight. *She must be the cook*, he thought. He was right …

THIRTY-FIVE

SAINT VERAN, FRANCE.

March 25, 2031.

The pine trees were beginning to thin out, exposing her to the latest round of blustering wind and snow. She stopped for a moment to rest and catch her breath. Leaning against one of the massive trunks to shield herself from the relentless onslaught of the elements, she surveyed the area. It was well below -30 °F, and she worried about frostbite. *How far had she traveled? Seven miles from camp, give or take?* She had to push onward. She knew when they awoke and discovered she had escaped with their food supplies they would track her down. Icy needles stabbed at her face as she moved away from her temporary shelter.

The dull light of the moon broke through the snow-filled ash clouds followed by a streak of lightning and a boom of thunder loud enough to make her clap her hands over her ears. Snow, ash, thunder, lightning, and no rain were the new norm for this horrible world.

Lightning flashed again, revealing a building in the distance. She hoped it might provide her with temporary shelter and food. Leaving the safety of the tree line, she noticed there was a road paved with smooth stone beneath the deep snow and ash. Each time lightning lit up the sky, she used it to guide her way to the large chateau. Wary of attracting attention, her steps along the road were inaudible. She knew the group of men she had belonged to would not be here, but there were others, and she had no intention of meeting up with any of them. They liked to use what few women were left in this world for cooking, skinning the meat, and other unmentionable things. She hated their touch, their lust. She pulled her black shroud tightly around her face. She had to get inside, if only for an hour.

After peering inside the windows and not seeing any signs of life, she padded slowly up the steps to the impressive front door made of carved wood and standing over eight feet tall. She pushed on it gently, and it moved under the pressure. Leaning into it, the door swung open without so much as a creak. She struck one of her few remaining matches and made a torch out of a bundle of sticks and brush she had gathered. Her makeshift light revealed a large foyer with walls covered in rich tapestries. Family portraits stared down at her, accusing her of being an intruder. Making her way through the large hall, she noticed a door ajar. The door swayed easily when she walked through it, and her small flame revealed a spotless, gleaming kitchen.

A scampering sound froze her mid-step. She caught a glimpse of the small cupboard door closing beneath the kitchen sink. Withdrawing her knife and clutching it in her left hand, she opened the cabinet door with care. A child peered out at her eyes wide in terror.

Sheathing her knife and crouching down, she said, 'Who are you, child?'

The child did not answer.

'I will not hurt you. See? My knife is put away. Tell me who are you?'

Clementina maneuvered herself as far back into the corner of the crawlspace as she could, but there was no escape. 'My name is Clementina, or Clem,' she replied in a quivering voice.

'Where are your parents?'

Clem sobbed with despair. 'Mother and Father are dead upstairs in the bed with my sister, Sophie.'

'You, poor child. Are you all alone in this world like me?'

There was no reply from the little girl, and the woman started to repeat her question, but a small tinny voice said, 'Yes.'

'We can be friends, then. Do you live here?'

Clem crawled forward a few inches, peered at the stranger dressed in a black-hooded cloak, and shivered. 'You won't hurt me, will you?'

'No, little one. I will not hurt you.'

'Do you promise?'

'I promise. Please answer my question. Do you live here?'

'Yes. All my life.'

'Is there any food left in this great home of yours?'

'Not anymore. I finished the last of it two days ago, but I found some nuts outside. I have them here in my pocket if you would like to share.'

'Thank you, Clem. That is very kind of you. Can you come out where I can see you, so I do not have to bend over to talk to you.'

'Remember, you promised you would not hurt me.'

'I remember my promise to you. Give me your hand, and I will help you, so you do not bump your head on the way out.'

The minute they touched hands Clem threw her small arms around the woman's neck in a warm embrace.

* * *

The woman, with Clem following closely behind, went outside to build a small fire to cook the last of the stolen food. Morning was trying to break through, but the snow and ash continued to fall. The woman placed several large rocks around a hole she had dug in the frozen ground and built a small lean-to to shield the fire. Adding sticks and brush, she hit her flint against a flat rock and watched the sparks catch the brush aflame. Hands outstretched, Clem warmed herself while the woman withdrew meat from her backpack, stabbed two pieces with some sticks, and held them over the fire to cook.

'You could have cooked the meat inside. We have many fireplaces.'

The woman gave her a sideways glance. 'I feel more at home being outside.'

'It has been a long time since I had anything cooked to eat,' Clem said with a touch of wonder in her small voice.

The woman rose to her feet and eyed the distant ridgeline and woods around them. 'How long have you been alone, child?'

'Since Christmas.'

The woman stood shell-shocked. 'It is the end of March. You have been alone for three months?' She paused. 'What have you been eating since December?'

Clem hesitated and gazed longingly at the meat sizzling on the sticks. 'When Father heard the stories about the disease spreading across Europe, he went into town with Nathan and Bryan and brought all the food and water from our grocery store to our basement in the middle of the night.'

The woman's eyes narrowed into slits, and her tone changed. '*Who* are Nathan and Bryan?'

Something about the woman's voice was different, and it frightened her. 'They were two of Father's workers who took care of the fields and the chickens. They both used to live above the barn, but ...,' she swallowed nervously, 'they don't live there anymore.'

The woman's voice softened. She could tell she had scared the child and needed to be more careful. 'Where are they now? Nathan and Bryan?'

Clem looked at the woman's face, and then back at the meat. 'Can we eat now?'

'Of course, child. Just as soon as you tell me about Nathan and Bryan.'

'Father said that they both got sick.' She cast her eyes down and grew pensive.

'What is wrong, Clem? Finish what you were saying and then we can eat.'

'I never saw them get sick. One night, I heard Mother and Father arguing. I never heard them argue before, and it scared me. They were talking about Nathan and Bryan, and Father said in a loud voice that he had to do it to keep our family safe. He said we could not share our food with them, or anyone. There wasn't enough as it was. Then I heard Mother start to cry.'

186

'I am sorry, Clem. I know how hard it is to relive painful memories.'

'Father said we would be safe in our home because the village was three miles away.' She wiped her eyes and nose with a dirty tissue she pulled out of the front pocket of her dress.

'We aren't safe. No one is.' The woman turned the meat to roast it on the other side. They would have to go back inside soon. She passed one of the meat sticks to the little girl.

Clem held it out in front of her lips, blowing on it to cool it off. Her mouth was watering as she took her first bite. It was still hot, but she thought that nothing had ever tasted so good. 'It's delicious,' she said between bites. 'What kind of meat is it?'

The woman ignored the question. "I am happy you like it. How did your family get sick?'

Clem took another small bite and chewed it thoughtfully. With tear-filled eyes, she said, 'Father went into the woods to chop down a tree for Christmas Eve. When he came back inside, I overheard him tell Mother that the forest was full of the biggest rats he had ever seen. That night, Father started to cough up blood, and Mother helped him into bed. He died the next morning; Mother and Sophie died in bed with him two days later. I covered them with a sheet and blanket and prayed over them.' She looked into the fire. 'But I am not so sure God answers prayers anymore, if He ever did to begin with.'

* * *

She scanned the tree line one final time. The blizzard-like conditions were covering all her tracks, and she knew if the men were searching for her, they would need to seek shelter ... she was safe for the time being. 'Let's go inside, child. We can finish eating by one of those fireplaces you mentioned. Do you have chopped wood inside?'

'Oh yes. Father filled the library with plenty of firewood. That is where I sleep at night.'

They walked inside the manor, and Clem led the way into the massive library. The woman gaped in awe; she had never seen so many books in one place. The walls were made of heavy wooden panels, museum-grade paintings hung from every angle she looked, and a large, stone fireplace dominated the back of the room. Huge stacks of wood had been positioned on the marble floor, enough to last for many months. The woman added several large pieces to the hot coals; a blazing fire roared to life and soon warmed the entire room. They ate the remainder of the meat in silence, listening to the howl of the wind and the crackling of burning logs. Clem yawned and laid down near the fireplace, staring into the flames.

'Are you sleepy, child?'

Yawning a second time, she said, 'I am. Are you?'

The woman laid down next to her and covered them both up with the heavy blankets.

Clem looked into the woman's eyes. 'You won't hurt me, will you?'

'No, little one, I will not hurt you.'

'Do you promise?'

'I promise.'

'I'm glad you were the one to find me. I trust you.' Clem gave the woman a gentle kiss on her cheek and closed her eyes.

'I am glad I was the one to find you, too. Go to sleep, little one.'

Outside, in the distance, lightning etched the sky, and the gray ash continued to fall.

* * *

The snow had stopped, but the sky was an ugly shade of slate gray. The men would be on the move, and they were all excellent trackers. Her backpack was heavy on her shoulders again. She did not feel any sadness for what she had done – the child had meant nothing to her.

There was a well-used trail behind the manor, and she walked it at a brisk pace. Her stomach was full, and she had no doubt she could outdistance the men. She smiled. They would never have her again ... never force her to satisfy their dark desires.

Looking down at the path, she saw the depression in the ground half a second before she stepped on it. A deadfall right in the middle of the trail. The trap was set by the child's father to protect his family and his home. She fell through the branches and boughs onto the sharpened stakes below. She looked up at the darkening sky and the latest snow fall. *The men will never have their way with me again.* Closing her eyes, the snow buried her in its wet embrace ...

THIRTY-SIX

DEFIANCE, IOWA.

June 10, 2031.

Will Bennett was a survivalist. Some of the folks around his hometown called people like him *doomsday preppers*. But he preferred the term *survivalist* because that was what he was doing right now ... surviving in his bunker.

He was mocked with nicknames such as *Crazy Willie* or *retard*. That latter one hurt, but he guessed it had some truth to it. They considered him a loon for stocking up on water and canned goods; they laughed right in his face whenever he showed up at the gun and ammo store. Sometimes, he was pushed or even punched. No one was laughing now. It was quite possible he was the only person alive in Defiance or the whole state of Iowa, for that matter, except for others of his kind. He knew a few of them: survivalists usually kept to themselves but talked with each other about generators, food storage solutions, water, and air purifiers. At the world's end, it was better to have too much than too little, he surmised.

Theories ran the gamut of how it would happen from nuclear war to zombies, but he believed it would end by God's design. His mother, a religious woman who had attended church daily, spoke of the Horsemen of the Apocalypse riding forth to bring death, famine, and plague upon all – an angel heralding their arrival by trumpet; *damn it all to hell, she had been right.* After listening to his mother, he started working on a bunker. He had zero desire to meet up with those horrific seven horsemen of his mother's belief.

When she died eight years ago from a liver-eating cancer, his father pulled him out of school and put him to work at the family's gas station; he said school was a waste of time for someone like Will, someone with no gray matter to speak of. Will knew he was not very smart, if he were being truthful – he was being too kind to himself, and he always told the truth. Though his pa often told him he was as dumb as a rock and hurt him with his hard words, Will was good at building things with his hands, and his dad *reluctantly* complimented his carpentry skills once.

The underground bunker was his pride and joy and took him over a year to build all by his lonesome with no help from anyone: a secret place of his own. Will used his father's backhoe to dig a long, deep trench into which he buried an old shipping container that was twenty feet long and eight feet wide, plenty big enough for him to reside in comfortably. Once he was satisfied with his living arrangements, he began stockpiling it with everything he required for the long haul and what other survivalists told him he would need in the inevitable end.

He looked over at the chalkboard near his bunk. He marked it with an X for every day he believed had passed. Not being able to see the sun or the moon made it difficult to determine, but he did his best. According to the X's on the board, it had been nearly six months since the eruption and that thing they called a *nuclear winter. Did the plague ever reach America?* He hoped it hadn't, but whatever the case, he was getting lonely being underground all the time with no one to talk to. Furthermore, he was almost out of food and water, so he decided it was time to have a look above ground. *Just a peek, mind you.*

Will stepped out of the entrance to his container and made his way up the long dirt tunnel he had braced with wood. The hatch was his only entrance to the outside world. He unlocked his father's old padlock he used to secure himself safely inside, smiling at his smart thinking. After removing the lock, he pushed at the hatch – it did not budge *at all*. Using his shoulder, he braced himself and threw his body weight into it. Over and over, he pushed at the hatch, panic mounting. The only result was dirt and ash falling onto his face and clothing. He was buried inside with no way of escape. With a sense of dread, he trudged back to his bunker. Sitting on his bed, he pulled his stuffed bear close to him and wondered how long it would take for him to starve to death.

THIRTY-SEVEN

PETROPAVLOVSK-KAMCHATSKY, RUSSIA.

September 15, 2031.

Head bowed, he sat cross-legged in the center of the street he had grown up on. His right hand pillowed by the deep gray ash; his left hand squeezed into a tight fist and pressed hard against his forehead. There was a rifle with a scope at his feet and a shotgun strapped across his broad back. Two handguns and several large hunting knives were tied around his waist completed his arsenal. He raised his head slowly and looked once more upon the ruins of his city.

Nothing was left: every window was broken, cars and trucks were turned over and set on fire, houses and businesses as far as he could see were burned to the ground. He had discovered multiple mass graves while doing reconnaissance – the corpses were burned beyond recognizing man from woman. Some of the bodies appeared to be in the throes of death with hands and arms outstretched, mouths open in a silent scream of agony. The city had tried to stop the plague by burning the dead and those suspected of carrying the disease. *A horrible way to die.* Aside from the graves, he found bodies in their homes, hiding in closets or under beds. Those not burned had their bones picked clean by animals ... and humans, based on the teeth marks.

As a hunter, he had seen many animals taken down by a wolf or bear and eaten alive. Even for a man such as he, it was not a pleasant sight to behold, no matter how many times he had witnessed it. *Was that how these poor souls had died?* He knew man was more of a primal beast than any animal. Perhaps he was not alone after all. *In this new world, had man taken to eating man?* He would have to be on his guard.

* * *

For the past year, his home was the inside of an abandoned air-raid bunker, deep underground in a deserted warehouse. A holdover from the cold war, he assumed. Two days ago, he left his safehold and walked the streets of his neighborhood, hoping – *no that was the wrong word to use* – praying for some sign of life. He found nothing: no dogs, no cats, not even a bird in the sky. He walked inside every grocery store, and all were completely ransacked. Any food containers left behind were ripped apart by madmen, and all canned goods were gone. He was a brave man, a strong man; however, looking around him now, tears filled his eyes. His father mentioned once that loneliness, a complete lack of love and friendship, was the most painful way to die, more so than anything else imaginable. His father knew this better than most for he spent many years in the solitary cells of the Gulag prison camps for his unfavorable political viewpoints.

* * *

Exiting the last store, he entered an alleyway. Looking to his left, a small body was burned beyond recognition. *Where was the child's mother and father when this happened? There were no answers anymore ... what was the point of asking questions of a dead world?* A sound from his back-right side startled him. He grabbed for his rifle and silently pivoted on his heels.

'Hello? Who is there?'

No answer.

Had it been his imagination? He heard a second noise coming from his left side, several yards in front of him. No, it had not been his imagination. And then he saw it: a black rat, the kind suspected of carrying the plague ... the *Black Death*. This explained the teeth marks he had seen on the bodies. Very slowly, he dropped to one knee and brought his rifle to eye level. As he slid his finger over the trigger, a cacophony of grinding teeth filled the alley behind him. He lowered the rifle and swung his head around to look over his shoulder. Hundreds of huge black and brown rats were everywhere he looked: on top of overturned cars, on garbage cans, at every window, at every door. He swung his rifle upside-down and pointed the opening of the barrel under his chin. He refused to witness his own death of being eaten alive.

THIRTY-EIGHT

VATICAN CITY, ROME, ITALY.

December 21, 2031.

Father Camassei stood on the Papal balcony, looking down on St. Peter's Square. Though it was nightfall, all Rome had been in total darkness for over a year. *How long had he been alone?* The days and the nights blurred into one with no beginning and no end. His food and water were running dangerously low, and he wondered, not for the first time, how much more of his precious life was left. He questioned whether he should end it or not. All he had to do was lean over the balcony and let go, but suicide was a grave sin, though it was not his true reason for continuing to live. He was terrified of what was waiting for him in death. He remembered the old woman's words, 'Hell fire is where you will spend eternity.' There was no escaping the truth, especially after what he had done.

The pounding on the outer doors of the Sistine Chapel and the pleading cries from the few survivors to be let in and given refuge within the church still haunted him. He refused to answer the door and kept it locked tightly. He, Father Joseph Camassei, had turned his back on his flock, not wanting to share what food and water he had left. His greatest moment of weakness. When he had finally opened the door, they were gone. Those seeking his help were surely dead, and he was to blame. He would burn in Hell for that sin; he was certain.

He reflected on the last days when the plague was sweeping across Europe unchecked. Pope Nicholas and Cardinal Borgogni died quickly, both succumbing to the disease within a few hours of becoming ill. There would never be another Pope. He turned around, away from the square. Pope Nicholas lay on the Papal bed in front of him, a simple white shroud covered his body. When the plague struck, no one wanted to touch any corpse, not even the Pope's. This was the only burial Pope Nicholas would ever receive.

He picked up his candle and went back inside the Papal apartment, thinking Pope Nicholas was one of the lucky ones. With few exceptions, the dead were left to rot wherever they had fallen, even those inside the Vatican.

* * *

He stood in the bitter cold with his arms folded across his chest, surveying St. Peter's Square in front of him. His black cloak and hood provided little warmth against the icy wind. He hated this place and everything the Catholic Church stood for. His mother died giving birth to him. The fact she was not married at the time made her guilty of sin in the eyes of the church, and she had not been absolved of it prior to her death. He shook his head, the anger of the memory mounting within his soul. This night was about food and revenge.

His followers appeared out of the mist of swirling black ash, flanking him on both sides. There were fourteen men and three women. If they found no food, one of his weakest men would be sacrificed. They all knew the dirty truth of survival; they had done it before and were fine with doing it again. No one ever expected to be the chosen one, but he always made sure the sacrifice had no knowledge of his impending death by killing him quickly from behind.

He hoped the Vatican had food. Afterward, they would destroy everything within and then set the place on fire. He smiled at the thought of it.

A dim flickering light cast by a single candle in one of the balconies caught his attention. He would not have to kill one of his men after all.

***

He knelt by the bedside of Pope Nicholas and said a prayer of forgiveness. *With no one left to hear his confession, would God hear his prayer?*

The old woman still harassed him in his nightmares. Soon after the plague struck, he went to her bedchamber. The four Swiss guards standing watch outside her door were dead. He tried to convince himself that they died of the plague, but there were no signs of the disease on any of them: no blackness covering their bodies and no swelling of their limbs. They were just dead, lying in the hallway with a look of horror written on their faces. He opened her door, knowing the room would be empty. Everything was in its place and the outline of her body was pressed deeply into the mattress, but she was gone.

One night while he was looking down onto the square, not long after she disappeared, a feeling of dread overcame him. He witnessed a small, bent-over figure like that of the old woman walking across the cobblestones. The person stopped and tilted her head up to gaze at the balcony where he stood. No face was visible beneath the hood, but he knew it was her. A moment later, she vanished into the falling ash, and he wondered if it were all a dream.

***

He no longer saw the flame of the candle, but it was not important. First, they had to get inside. He motioned for his men to spread out and find a way in.

***

He finished his prayer and stood up with great difficulty, using his cane to support his weight. He was tired and hungry. Exiting the Papal apartment, he shuffled along the dark hallway, holding his candle out in front of him to light his way. He had only taken several steps when he heard the muffled sound of glass breaking. He wondered if he should hide. *No, someone might need my help.*

He refused to make the mistake of turning his back on his flock again. Perhaps God was giving him a second chance – *the Lord heard my prayer.* His hip was in pure agony as he quickened his pace, but he felt strangely exhilarated. *I have been given a second chance.* He heard a footfall behind him and went to turn but darkness descended upon him.

* * *

When he blinked his eyes open, his head was pounding, and he tasted blood. There were voices nearby and the sound of a hammer hitting something. His vision was blurred as he tried to focus on his surroundings. He was lying face down on the floor, and his wrists were tied behind his back. Someone knelt next to him and raised his head.

'Awake now, Priest?'

Father Joseph looked into the eyes of the man speaking to him. The man was dressed in a black cloak, his face was hidden by the hood he wore, but his eyes were visible. In those eyes he saw only hatred. 'Why did you hit me and tie me up, my son? I can help you.'

'I am not your son, old man. As far as helping us, well, I can assure you that you will.' The man stood up and walked away.

Father Joseph laid his cheek back down on the cold marble and tried to fathom what was happening. He was in the main hallway leading into the Sistine Chapel. The sound of banging and something being pried from the wall continued. There were muffled voices, but he could not discern what was being said.

The noise stopped, and he heard the footsteps of several men approaching him. Pulling him to his feet, they dragged him into the chapel. Above him, Father Joseph glimpsed *The Last Judgement* by Michelangelo di Lodovico Buonarroti Simoni. A large crucifix once holding a life-sized figure of Jesus Christ had been pried from a corner wall. The figure of Christ laid on the floor, broken into pieces by the hammer.

The hooded man knelt next to him. 'You said that you wanted to help us, Priest. Now, you shall. As your savior, Jesus Christ, was hung from the cross until his death, so shall you. And when you are dead, we will eat of your body and drink of your blood.'

THIRTY-NINE

SOMEWHERE IN AMERICA.

March 28, Easter Sunday, Year of Our Lord, 2032.

They were starving. He and his two brothers were huddled around the small campfire, lost in their own thoughts. Even though their faces were hidden, he knew their fears because he had the same ones. They were afraid of the scarcity of their food source, and they had every right to be scared. They knew the ramification of finding no more prey to hunt: brother against brother. In the beginning, there had been eleven men in his small group.

They were down to three.

He stood, walked away from the fire, and was swallowed up by the shadows of the surrounding forest. The weather was changing again and getting colder. Most nights, the temperature dipped below -30 °F. Even if they found enough food to sustain them, how long could they survive in the plummeting temperature? The bitter windchill made his chest hurt with every breath. Searching the sky for guidance, he brushed away the ash and frost from his goggles, his black cloak billowed around him. Turning toward his brothers, he gathered them for the hunt. They extinguished the campfire with snow, picked up their backpacks and weapons, and prepared for their trek. Each man had his own personal preference of weaponry: bow and arrow, handgun or rifle, Bowie knife, or machete. They moved off at a fast pace into the woods; the hunt for their prey was on.

The landscape was a barren wasteland of twisted stumps and burnt brush with a swamp to their left and dense, weathered evergreens to their right. The swamp was a dangerous place for anyone, even in the best of times, and the evergreens were foreboding. Below him, he saw the reflection of ice over water and turned in that direction with his two brothers trailing on his heels. A small shack came into view, a thin tendril of smoke wafting lazily from its chimney.

Inside was the last civilized man alive. *The three brothers did not know this fact. How could they?*

They made their way silently toward the cabin.

* * *

Within a few days, two of the brothers turned against the weakest – then brother against brother.

EPILOGUE

HEAVEN.

Eternity.

The Lord our God looked down upon the earth, and He saw His work was done. He reached out His left hand and swept the ash from the sky, clearing it like it was in the beginning. He calmed the oceans and the seas, the waters becoming still once more. Reaching out His right hand, the plague covering every corner of the earth was cleansed from the land.

Satan asked, 'When will you forgive them of their sins?'

God looked at Satan and said in a voice like a thousand thunder claps, 'Never.'

Satan looked down upon the earth and smiled. 'Let us begin our game, anew.'

* * *

For this End was only a new beginning. It would happen again, and again, and again.

For some sins are never forgiven...

Some punishments eternal...

THE END.

ABOUT THE AUTHOR

THOMAS SMITH served in the United States Marine Corps from 1975-1979. He was a member of the last Marine unit to stand guard at the National Security Agency (N.S.A.) in Fort Meade, Maryland, from 1976-1978. From there, he was stationed in Okinawa, Japan, until his honorable discharge in 1979. Afterward, he lived in Licola, Italy, for three years, traveling extensively throughout Europe. He was a member of the Monmouth County, N.J. Sheriff's Department for twenty-six years, retiring in 2013. He is the proud father of three children and one grandchild: Ashley, Caroline, Brian, and Bayne.

The events described in chapter five are accurate. On March 18, 1998, while serving with the Sheriff's department, Thomas walked in on an armed robbery in Long Branch, N.J. One handgun was aimed at his forehead and another was placed against his back: between a rock and a hard place. He was taken into a rear storeroom, hogtied, and relieved of his service weapon as the two men whispered about killing him. There is more to the story, but those memories will never be revealed or shared with anyone. That dangerous and intense situation planted the seed for *The End*.

SHANNON GAMBINO ... mama of two incredible teenagers, Marine Corps Veteran, IT consultant, author, editor, professional bikini and athletic bodybuilder, outdoor enthusiast.

Shannon lives every day of her life to the fullest, immersing herself in life's beauty and eclectic charm.

Make memories, share tales, love others ... live. ~ S.G.

www.ingramcontent.com/pod-product-compliance
Lightning Source LLC
Chambersburg PA
CBHW060433180626
46817CB00007B/2792